BRINGING UP
BEAUTY

SYLVIA McNICOLL

Stoddart Kids
TORONTO • NEW YORK

Acknowledgements

Sylvia McNicoll would like to thank the Ontario Arts Council for assisting in her own personal disaster recovery; Diane Thurner for sharing her "bringing up Dudley" stories; and Canine Vision Canada for showing her the ending.

We acknowledge for their financial support of our publishing program the Government of Canada through the Book Publishing Industry Development Program (BPIDP), the Canada Council, and the Ontario Arts Council.

First published as trade paperback in 1994
by Maxwell Macmillan Canada

Published in Canada in 1999 by
Stoddart Kids,
a division of Stoddart Publishing Co. Limited
34 Lesmill Road
Toronto, Canada M3B 2T6
Tel (416) 445-3333 Fax (416) 445-5967
E-mail Customer.Service@ccmailgw.genpub.com

Published in the United States in 2000 by
Stoddart Kids,
a division of Stoddart Publishing Co. Limited
180 Varick Street, 9th Floor
New York, New York 10014
Toll free 1-800-805-1083
E-mail gdsinc@genpub.com

Distributed in Canada by
General Distribution Services
325 Humber College Blvd.
Toronto, Canada M9W 7C3
Tel (416) 213-1919 Fax (416) 213-1917
E-mail Customer.Service@ccmailgw.genpub.com

Distributed in the United States by
General Distribution Services
85 River Rock Drive, Suite 202
Buffalo, New York 14207
Toll free 1-800-805-1083
E-mail gdsinc@genpub.com

Canadian Cataloguing in Publication Data

McNicoll, Sylvia, 1954-
Bringing up Beauty

ISBN 0-7736-7479-9

I. Title.

PS8575.N52B7 1999   jC813'.54   C99-930791-6
PZ7.M35Br 1999

Cover illustration: Sharif Tarabay
Cover design: Tannice Goddard

Printed and bound in Canada

For Bob
who has more than a few things in common
with Elizabeth's dad.

Chapter 1

"I'm not going to love you."

The ugly black puppy sitting in front of me cocked her head and looked right at me, dog-eyed honest. Caramel-coloured eyes she had, and they asked me questions I couldn't answer, or maybe just didn't want to. Her slightly folded ears lifted and the fur around her forehead bunched, making her look worried. But it was the paw she placed on my arm that really slayed me—like a size thirteen shoe on a three-month-old baby. It put a weight on me, a trust, that made me try to explain to her.

I took the paw in my hand and shook it. "We can be friends, sure. But this is only for a year or so—I can't love you."

She bounded forward, nipping at my hand with her pointed puppy teeth.

"NO!" I commanded, yanking my hand away. "That hurts!" She was only teething on me but it wouldn't do for the special dog she was to become. My mother walked into the kitchen as the puppy was washing my face with her flapjack tongue.

"Getting acquainted, Elizabeth? That's nice," Mom said as she immediately headed for the bulletin board where she kept her list of things to do.

"What are we going to call her?" I asked.

"Beauty," Mom answered, ticking something off on the list. She took a cucumber from the vegetable bin in the refrigerator and started to peel it.

"For a black Lab! That's a wussy name. And I thought this was a family project—we should all get a vote." For a moment the unfairness of it twisted up my insides, making me angry. We'd all agreed it was a good idea to raise a puppy for Canine Vision Canada, but somehow on paper I'd forgotten the dog would be alive. It didn't seem right to make a project of her now that she was in front of me, wriggling, squirming, jumping and licking. And although the whole family had agreed on fostering the puppy, I wanted to blame Mom because she'd gone ahead and named the dog.

"Besides," I added, "this puppy is ugly."

Mom finished with the cucumber and stuck the peels on her face, her environmental skin treatment. "She has inner beauty, Elizabeth."

I made a face. It was something Mom might have told me if I'd asked if I was beautiful. With wiry, copper-coloured hair and long white eyelashes, how could I be? But my mother's voice smiled and those cucumber peels looked like a crazy war paint smeared across her forehead, her chin and over her nose. I could feel the twisting anger melt. And I realized that I liked this puppy for being ugly—it gave us something in common. Plus my parents had called me a stupid name too, after the Queen. I argued some more anyway.

"C'mon Mom. Why not Rambo or even Beast?"

"Actually, she came with the name." Mom removed the peels from her face, one by one, dropping them in an ice cream container. "Lucinda's Beauty Parlour sponsored her and asked that she be called Beauty. Seems they got the idea from the local fire hall. The dogs they sponsor are all called Smokey." Mom held out the container full of egg shells, rusting apple cores, coffee grinds, and now her environmental skin pack. "Would you empty this into the compost, please? "

"Aw, why me?" I groaned. I hate anything to do with the compost pile, Mom's last family project.

"Because it's your planet we're trying to save."

"Yeah right. It doesn't belong to Debra or Dad."

"Your sister and your father aren't here right now or I might ask them." She pressed the container into my hands. Another tick on her list of things to do. "Oh, and Elizabeth."

"What now, Mom?"

"Take Beauty with you. Put the leash on her first, though. Remember what the training manual said."

"Everything by the book," I grumbled as I hitched Beauty to the six-foot leash. "Outside," I told the puppy.

"Say it with authority," Mom suggested. Easy for her, she's a teacher.

"OUTSIDE," I repeated, this time in an army general's voice. Together we headed for the bin in the back corner of the yard, Beauty almost backflipping beside me in between yanking and chewing at the leash.

I suppose I should have set the ice cream container down instead of propping it between my legs and the compost bin, but I'm always in too much of a hurry when there's anything to do with compost.

I used my only free hand to lift the lid. A million potato bugs scurried over a growing heap of unrecognizable food scraps. I wanted to scratch myself all over. I wanted to throw up at the sight of the rotting food. I wanted to throw the lid back on quickly. But in the heartbeat that it took to fight my nausea, Beauty yanked the leash hard. That made me shift my legs which in turn made the ice cream container spill over, dumping future compost on one sneaker and jean leg.

"Aw gross," I said. I bent over and Beauty thought I wanted to play. She woofed and bounded back and forth. "No!" I yelled. "SIT! SIT!" Tucking the leash handle under my remaining clean sneaker, I shook my compost-covered foot over the bin, hoping and praying potato bugs couldn't fly. Then I scooped the other spillage back into the container, dumped it into the bin and slammed the lid.

With that job behind me, I turned to Beauty. "Hurry up!" I said, the command we'd chosen from the puppy manual for going to the bathroom. "HURRY UP!" I repeated, this time in the army general's voice.

But it was obvious Beauty hadn't read the manual. She cocked her head again with that same worried look and those same questions in her eyes. Somehow she came up with the wrong answer as she started growling and chewing at my sneakers.

"NO!" I said. "Hurry up!" I stayed in the same place, tapping my foot. Beauty still didn't get it. She picked up a stick in her mouth, and since that was allowed, I watched until she dropped it somewhere close to me. Then I grabbed the stick and threw it a little ways for her. "Fetch!"

Snatching it up, she danced around trying to break free of the leash. I tugged her closer to me. She shook the stick with her head, inviting me to wrestle her for it. "Sit!" I told her, placing my hand firmly on her hindquarters. "Sit! Sit! Sit I said!" Finally she lowered herself completely to the ground. I grabbed her muzzle and gently pried the stick from her mouth.

Ten more times I threw the stick. Ten more times I forced it from her mouth. I gave up on getting her to sit. By the time we went in, Beauty hadn't once dropped the stick willingly in my hand. And she still hadn't "hurried up" either.

I was ready to escape into my room and leave her with Mom. She was energy draining, like Marnie, the four-year-old next door whom I sometimes babysit. I wasn't happy with what Mom told me next.

"Teresa called. Her bronchitis is worse so I'm teaching her class tonight."

"Aw no."

"Well, the lesson she had planned is so straightforward I can fill in without any class prep. It seemed a shame to cancel it on such short notice when so many students would show up anyway." Mom put her hands on my shoulders, her brow wrinkling the way Beauty's had earlier. "Be a good girl, Elizabeth, and look after Beauty."

"I don't have time to be a good girl right now—I have the G.A.D tonight."

"The what?"

"You know, my Get Acquainted Dance at Centennial."

"Oh right, I forgot. Dad or Debra should be home before then. Just be sure and crate Beauty if you have to leave before they arrive."

I slumped into a kitchen chair staring at the mutt as Mom rushed around us getting ready. "Your father's supper is in the microwave. He just has to nuke it for, oh, say fifty seconds and then check it again. Debra's probably eaten, but if not, there's more leftovers in the fridge." Mom threw on her coat. "Oh, and there's an empty peanut butter jar and a Chocotella jar for you to scrub and put in the recycling." Mom kissed me and stooped down to pat Beauty. "Bye," she called as she headed out the door.

"Ha, she's gone, Beauty," I said as the car drove away. I grabbed the two gooey jars standing in the sink and stuck them in the trash, covering them up with meat scraps and other unrecyclables. "There. I saved a lot of energy that way." I rubbed my hands together and Beauty tilted her head. "Oh, don't look at me like that. It takes a lot of hot water and scrubbing to get peanut butter and Chocotella off so I'm sure it's just as good for the planet this way. Right?" The puppy still looked doubtful. I changed the subject. "Next thing we're going to do is put you in the crate so I can take my bath in peace." I picked her up and carried her to the cage in the corner of the kitchen.

Mom had covered the bottom with a piece of fun fur left over from a past Halloween costume. Beauty's water and food dish sat in one corner. I tossed a couple of milk bone treats into the dish and before she could finish them, slammed the cage door.

I ran upstairs and turned on the bath taps full blast, dumping a couple capfuls of Mom's Seafoam bubble bath into the water. "I'm too sexy for my shirts, too sexy for my shirts, so sexy that it hurts," I sang as I danced into Debra's room and opened her closet door. Every piece of clothing hanging there was black except for the one thing I wanted. Yes! Her purple silk shirt beckoned to me, clean and pressed. I grabbed it and danced back into the bathroom to hang it on the back of the door. "Too sexy for my jeans, too sexy for my jeans, whatever sexy means." Whatever it meant, I had a fair idea I wasn't sexy but I also didn't care much either. I gathered up my jeans and hunted under my bed for my favourite purple suede desert boots. A bunch of dirty socks, an old chocolate bar wrapper, and a wasteland of dust bunnies were growing there, but no boots. They were in my closet. One last matching pair of purple socks dangled from two separate drawers. The gods were on my side.

Back in the bathroom, I draped my clothes over the toilet seat and placed my socks in my boots on the floor nearby. I stripped and sunk into the tub. The water covered me up to my shoulders. Sighing, I shut the taps and then lay back with my eyes closed.

That's when I heard Beauty. It started as a whining with a few yips and yaps in it. Then it grew into a whimpering that turned into full-blown howling, sort of a cross between a baby and a very sad wolf. I covered my ears and tried to ignore it. One long howl, now, penetrated into my very bones, making them vibrate, making me shudder.

I couldn't stand it. I got up out of the tub, draped a towel around me and drip, drip, dripped down the stairs. When I stood shivering and scowling in front of the cage, Beauty stopped crying immediately. She wagged her tail and shifted around on her front paws. I opened the cage door and she barked once in appreciation. Her flapjack tongue slathered all over my face as I bent down to pick her up.

"Okay, okay. We're both girls anyway." I hoisted her up and headed back for the bathroom. She weighed about as much as a jumbo sack of potatoes, but the potatoes wriggled and became even heavier as I walked. "You stay here and don't move," I told her as I finally let Beauty down. I sank back into the water and shut my eyes. A full tub, which Mom tells us never to use—she owed me that. The hot water lapped at my chin. It felt good, as though I was melting, soothing and peaceful.

Suddenly there was a scrambling, scratching noise on

the side of the tub. My eyes shot open in time to see the front end of Beauty hanging over into the water. I sat up quickly.

Too late. Her back end was in now too. The live potato sack landed on me.

"Beauty! What are you doing!" Her paws slipped and slid all over me, her nails leaving a trail of white crisscrosses on my skin. She started digging at the water, slopping little waves over the sides. "Ahhh! Get out!" I lifted her up and out of the tub. More water everywhere. "No don't!" I shouted as she started shaking herself all over Debra's shirt, my suede boots and everything else. To finish it all off, she "hurried up" on the floor.

A walking disaster, actually a waddling, pawing, swimming, shaking disaster. At that moment I was convinced it would be easy not to love Beauty.

Chapter 2

Mom doesn't buy disposable paper towels, which made wiping up Beauty's accident an even bigger pain. Naked, I leapt over the puddle and headed for the linen cupboard. I grabbed Mom's bag of cleaning rags and dumped a pile onto the floor to soak it up. "NO!" I said as I wiped up Beauty's mess. She watched me with her head to one side. Her confused look. "NO, NO, NO!" I repeated and Beauty shifted around on her paws. She wagged her tail. What should I do to make her understand? Probably take her outside, I thought, but I wasn't exactly dressed for the part. I dried the rest of the room with my bath towel and threw the rags into the laundry hamper. Then I scrambled into my soggy clothes and took Beauty out on her leash.

"Now hurry up," I told Beauty.

"RAWF!" she answered me back. It didn't work this time either. After ten minutes, I took her back in and she lay beside me in my room, still on the leash, as I blow-dried first Debra's silk blouse, then my boots and finally my hair. I tried blow-drying Beauty's fur but the machine frightened her right to the end of the leash under my bed.

"Come on out, will you please, Beauty. BEAUTY COME," I remembered my army general's voice. "I'm late as it is." She wouldn't budge.

I crossed my arms and thought for a moment. What did I have left to do? Makeup, which I needed to borrow from Debra, that was pretty much it. I changed my voice then to entice Beauty out. "Do you want to come see Debra's room? You'll like it, girl." Still no movement. I changed my voice again—"OUT, OUT, OUT!"—and dragged her from under the bed, across the floor, and down the hall into Debra's room.

"Nice eh?" I asked Beauty as I sat down at Debra's bureau. Although she dressed totally in black, Debra decorated her room totally in white. With a ricepaper window blind and a matching lamp shade on her desk lamp, one single poster on her walls, a sea gull against a blue sky with the words IF YOU LOVE IT, SET IT FREE underneath, Debra's room looked altogether just like Debra.

Her desk stood right next to the bureau, sloping downward, with her latest art project lying there alongside paint jars and brushes. Nine letter D's in separate squares painted in shades of pink and mounted on a board, simple, but beautiful. Debra again.

I kept Beauty's leash tight against me as I carefully searched through Debra's makeup drawer for what I wanted. Debra knew exactly how she arranged things, even though the makeup looked all a jumble. Stashed in among the lipsticks, powders, and eyeliner pencil was a foil-wrapped bundle. I picked it up. "Wonder what kind of makeup this is, eh girl?" Shaking it, I found the scrunched-up foil felt light, maybe even empty. I was dying to unwrap it but didn't dare.

There, the mascara. I was supposed to wait till I was thirteen to use any makeup, but with eyelashes like mine, I couldn't hold out any longer. I unscrewed the wand and carefully coated my lashes. A one hundred percent improvement. I read in Mom's *Chatelaine* magazine that if you coat your eyelashes again when they're dry, they'll look even thicker. I held the wand waiting. Beauty nudged me and I patted her, which made her jump up on me and knock the wand into the air. It landed on Debra's project.

"Oh no! Look what you made me do!" We're not supposed to say "Bad dog" but I sure felt like saying it. On one of Debra's perfect pink D's was a small fleck of black mascara. "I'll have to try to fix it," I told Beauty. I checked out the paints and picked the closest shade. Then I unscrewed the container and dabbed a little from the jar onto the canvas. The dab remained darker. Would Debra notice? Of course, Debra noticed everything, especially when it had anything to do with art. "We're as good as dead, Beauty." I closed the paint jar and rinsed out the brush.

"Oh well." I brushed on my second coat of mascara. At least I'd be a corpse with perfect eyelashes.

That's when Dad came in. Clunk! I heard his briefcase hit the floor. Every night it's that same noise he makes when he first arrives. Then a heavy sigh. "I'm home!" I heard him call.

"Hi Dad!" I called back. Now what? Should I cover my eyes with sunglasses and hope he didn't ask me why I needed them on in the house? Or should I chance him noticing the mascara? Dad was funny like that. A couple of years ago when I was crazy about *Find Waldo* books, he'd sit with me and help. He could always spot Waldo in among the millions of other little figures. He was like one of those computers he programs at work, searching quadrant one, no Waldo, searching quadrant two, no

Waldo, searching quadrant three, beep, beep, there's Waldo. But one day when I had my waist-length hair cut to my chin, Dad didn't notice.

"Where is everybody?" Dad asked.

Deciding to chance him without the sunglasses, I walked downstairs, Beauty in tow. "Mom's substitute teaching for Teresa. Debra is . . . well . . ." We both knew she was at her boyfriend Rolph's apartment.

"She knows how I feel about dating during the week," Dad interrupted. "Why can't she at least be at home for supper?"

Debra didn't come home for supper because she wanted to avoid the nagging. Instead, lucky me, I got to listen. I changed the subject. "Dad, could you give me a lift to school? There's a get acquainted dance that started five minutes ago."

"A dance on a school night?" Dad was looking straight into my eyes now. No comment on the mascara.

"C'mon Dad, the school decided the date, not me."

"I haven't even eaten."

"Well, if it weren't for the mutt here, I would have had time to walk." I only noticed now that Beauty had dragged my favourite stuffed animal down the stairs in her teeth. It was Igor, the purple monster that Scott, my longtime buddy next door, had given me for my tenth birthday. One glow-in-the-dark eye was already missing and Beauty seemed to be working on the remaining one. "Hey, where'd you get that? I haven't seen Igor in ages." I snatched my monster away and Beauty bounded forward, ready to tackle me for it.

"So this is the guide dog," Dad commented. It took him that long to notice a puppy. I couldn't believe I had worried about the mascara.

"Yeah Dad, could you maybe say hello to her later and drive me to school now?"

"Where are you going on a school night?"

"Da-aa-d, we've been through that. Mom would have driven me over to the dance by now if she hadn't agreed to teach Teresa's class. Beauty made a mess in the bathroom that I cleaned up so I'm late. . . ."

"I haven't even eaten yet."

I swear Dad's around computers too much. "Your dinner is in the microwave. You could eat afterwards."

"How long do I have to heat it?"

"Fifty seconds. Dad, I'm getting my jacket on."

"Oh, all right. Are we taking the dog? Where am I driving you again?"

"Dad!" Beauty and I scrambled into the van and Dad finally followed.

Beauty sat on the back seat, looking out and enjoying the ride. Beside her lay my purple monster—she'd managed to sneak Igor out with her.

Dad grumbled more about dances on school nights on the way to Centennial.

"They hold it on a school night so the dance doesn't go too late. Honestly Dad! I'll be home by nine-thirty."

"All right. Have a good time." We finally stopped discussing it as the van rolled up to the sidewalk in front of the school. Dad kissed my cheek and I dashed.

"Elizabeth!" he called just as I made it to the top of the stairs at the front door.

"Yeah Dad."

"How long was I supposed to microwave my supper for?"

"Fifty seconds!" I sighed, convinced Dad had used up every memory byte in his brain at the office.

♦   ♦   ♦

Arriving late for the dance made it really hard to find friends to hang around with. The gym was dark except for blue, green, red and yellow lights that pulsed across the room in time to the boom, boom, boom of the bass. Occasionally a face would be lit up in the eerie pulse but it was hard to recognize anyone in the blue or green flashes. Yellow wasn't too bad. I leaned against a wall thinking I'd watch for the yellow lights, but the wall was clammy wet, almost as though the gym itself was sweating from all the bodies inside. I stepped away quickly.

"Elizabeth!" a voice from the hall called.

I looked out and saw Alicia Jackson, my best friend. She was waving a bag of chips.

"Elizabeth, I need to ask you something!"

I stepped out of the gym towards Alicia.

"Here, want some chips? Sour cream and onion—bought them just for you." She held the bag out.

"Oh right, like they're not your favourite too." I grabbed a handful. "Thanks."

"Welcome. Scott's here." Alicia related this piece of information as though she'd just won a contest.

"Of course Scott is here. Grade eights were invited too and he told me he was coming."

"I know, but he's here." Grinning, breathless, she pointed towards a gym wall where a face temporarily lit up in blue looked somewhat like Scott's.

I smiled. Scott and I used to build forts together, and these days he always made the other guys let me play Rollerblade hockey with them. With my two best friends, this dance thing was going to be all right, even if I had arrived late in slightly soggy clothes. Maybe grade seven would turn out okay, too.

"So I need to know. Do you like Scott?" Alicia asked.

"What, are you crazy? Of course."

"No. I mean do you LIKE him."

"We're talking Scott, right? The guy who put raisins in his nose at my last birthday party and then snorted them out." I actually liked Scott for that. Alicia nodded, looking hopeful.

"Nah. I don't LIKE him the way you mean."

Alicia's eyes and face lit up then, as though one of those yellow bulbs had pulsed on from inside her. "So you won't mind if I ask him to dance?"

"Nah, why should I?"

"Great, let's go in."

I followed Alicia over to some of the new friends she'd made—she took different classes than I did this year. Vicky, Jessica and Lydia—she introduced the girls to me for the first time, but their names had been sprinkled through all her conversations lately.

They shouted over the loud music, starting and finishing each other's sentences, cracking up at jokes that I didn't get but pretended to anyway.

"This is for those who want to dance with that special someone," the disc jockey crooned into the mike as he put on a slow song.

Why should I mind, I asked myself when Alicia walked up to Scott, her hips swinging a little more than usual. Alicia's hair was blond and usually straight, but she'd tied a bouncy little ponytail off to one side and curled the ends of it and the rest of her hair. She wore wild cherry lip balm you could smell from three bodies away, and eye makeup she didn't even need. She grew thick black eyelashes entirely on her own and they made her eyes, which were a sort of swimming pool blue, look even bigger. She also wore a training bra and this year her breasts suddenly didn't need any more training.

The yellow light pulsed on her and Scott. Scott was taller than most of the boys at school, who all seemed to be the same height they were in grade four. He was thin and had a bony face and chocolate brown eyes. His hair was in one of those short angled cuts that made his head look bony too. I liked the way he looked, although I never thought about it much until the yellow light hit.

"They make a great couple, don't you think?" Vicky asked.

Was she really talking to me? I wondered. This was something new.

Blue, green, and then red pulsed on them. When Scott and Alicia were again spotlighted in yellow, I noticed for the first time the overbite Alicia was always complaining about. It made her mouth look puckered, as though it was ready for a kiss. I also noticed some dark hair growing on Scott's upper lip. That hair and Alicia's puckered lips bothered me for some reason.

The next time the yellow light hit them, I realized that even though Scott was taller, Alicia looked like she could pass for eighteen. Scott still looked like a kid, fuzzy moustache excepting.

"So are they a great couple or what?" Vicky asked me again.

They look bizarre together I thought, but just shrugged at her. "Yeah, sure, great."

As the red light flashed, Scott nodded and smiled and Alicia snuggled into his arms. *I don't LIKE him*, I told myself angrily, *why should I mind?* But now I had no one to talk to except Alicia's new friends, all giggling, clear-skinned beauties from another planet. Or was it me who was the alien observing earth life?

With only four slow dances the whole night, there were moments I actually did more than just observe. We all danced in circles and sometimes gangs, and once in a line that wound around the gym. I held onto Scott's back for that one. Alicia slow dancing with Scott made that suddenly feel incredibly weird. My hands felt tingly against his warmth. My face felt as though it was on fire.

But I still felt rotten enough not to want to drive home with Mrs. Jackson, especially when Alicia offered the three spaceketeers and Scott a lift too. As Alicia headed for the bathroom, I ducked into the pay phone at the front door.

"Hi, Dad?" I covered the receiver with my hand as I spoke.

"Elizabeth?" he asked groggily. I must have caught him napping.

"So Dad, have you eaten yet?" I was just bugging, but Dad didn't notice.

"Yes. Fifty seconds wasn't enough though. Supper was still cold."

"Uh huh. Dad, could you pick me up please?"

"Oh gosh, was I supposed to? Did I forget?"

"That's okay, Dad." I didn't feel like explaining about not wanting to drive with Alicia, so I let him believe I'd been waiting for him. "Can you come now, though? Quickly?"

Chapter 3

When I got home, Beauty was asleep in her crate curled up around my purple monster. Igor's other eye was missing now. Funny, as she lay there so peacefully, snout resting on purple polyester hair, I wanted suddenly to hug and pat her. I made a lot of noise getting milk from the fridge.

Beauty woke up. First her tail thumped slowly, a sleepy welcome. Then she came alive, wriggling and wagging so hard her body waved along with her tail. I opened the door of her crate, got down on the floor and let her lick me all over. It felt sloppy and wet, like a soaking washcloth lapping at my face. But it felt good too.

She placed her size thirteen paw on my arm and it didn't feel as heavy as it had earlier. I shifted it into my hand and shook it. "Friends, Beauty?" I said softly. I dropped her paw and went to the cupboard for some milk bones.

"Friends, Beauty?" I repeated and held out my hand. Beauty cocked her head, and asked me questions with her eyes. Then carefully she raised up her paw. "That's it, that's it, girl. Friends, friends," I urged.

The paw landed in my hand. "Good, Beauty!" I shook it and slipped Beauty a milk bone. "Outside?" I asked. Beauty sprang up as I jingled her leash. I snapped it onto her collar and she bounded alongside of me into the yard.

The air felt crisp and I could see my breath and the huge looming shadows Beauty and I were throwing under a full moon. There was a velvety soft silence except for the happy jingle of Beauty's leash as we jogged around to the side. Scott's house next door looked warm and inviting, with every window lit up. I noticed Mrs. Jackson's wagon pull into the driveway and I quickly turned away.

"FETCH!" I called out, becoming an army general again. I threw Beauty the stick twice and wrestled her for it both times.

At one point, she squatted and went to the bathroom. "HURRY UP!" I announced wildly. "HURRY UP," I repeated and slipped Beauty another milk bone.

"Da-aa-d," I called. "Da-aa-d!" I repeated as we ran inside. I wanted to share my exciting breakthrough with someone. Beauty had gone to the bathroom outside! I searched the ground floor for Dad and realized that, of course, Dad must be downstairs in the computer room. I hoisted Beauty up and rushed down the stairs. "Dad, Dad, guess what?"

He was sitting in front of a monitor with a telephone against his ear, obviously communicating with his home planet, Regal Trust. "Yes, on that abend on SOCK 1, override TRT53 dot M 2738101 with Roy 53 dot R.M2738101." "Well, then uncatalogue Roy 53 and throw it in again." "No?" Big sigh. "Okay, let's remove it and hold it till the morning. Goodnight." Click. Dad's eyes still scanned the computer screen.

"Dad, are you on call?" He hadn't been groggy from napping when I'd telephoned earlier. He'd been groggy from jumping back to that other dimension he goes into when he's concentrating on work.

"No. Just one of my projects." He looked my way. "Princess," he commented, out of the blue using my baby nickname. "You look . . . special tonight." He was scrutinizing my face, squinting. Noticing my mascara?

"Thanks Dad. I dressed up for the dance."

"They shouldn't have dances on school nights." His eyes drifted back to his monitor. "Did you want something, Elizabeth?"

"No, that's all right, Dad." It seemed pretty useless to try to talk to him now. I would have needed the Regal Trust pager to beep him back to me. "C'mon girl," I whispered to Beauty. "Time for bed."

◆　　　◆　　　◆

Next morning, I knew it would be my job to let Beauty out. Mom always slept in after teaching at night and Dad needed to return to his home planet.

I threw on some clothes and quickly snapped Beauty's leash onto her collar. "Hurry up!" I suggested, the moment we passed out the door. Grey with purple smudges of cloud, the sky glowed around the edges as though someone had just lit it with a match. There was a glistening of frost on the grass which was just melting into dew. Frost? In September. Weird, weird, weird, like everything else that was happening to me this year. Beauty sniffed around curiously. "C'mon, hurry up," I pleaded. "I have to go to school this morning."

Beauty found her stick and brought it to me. When I reached towards her, ready to force it from her mouth as usual, an amazing thing happened. She dropped the stick. "Yee haw!" I yelled. "Good dog, good Beauty." I threw it for her again. This time she wouldn't release it. Seven times

~ 20 ~

I threw it. Three times she dropped it near my hand. Four times, I wrestled her for it. Beauty was ahead one point. Still it was exciting.

"Hurry up," I suggested again. By now the entire sky had caught fire as the sun rose. Beauty cocked her head, her forehead wrinkling, her eyes questioning me as usual. "You know what I mean. Hurry up." I don't know if she understood or if she just needed to go, but Beauty looked around her and then squatted. "Yess! Good Beauty!" I fed her a milk bone. "We can go in for breakfast."

"You were in my room," Debra's flat voice announced. Lady Dracula, face powdered white, green eyes outlined in black, wearing tights, a ribbed turtleneck, a short skirt and clunky Doc Marten boots to match the outfit—she was awesome this morning, my sister Debra.

"Okay so I borrowed your shirt. It's not like you ever wear it and it's my favourite colour."

"Oh, so you borrowed my shirt too." Her flat voice sounded as though a pin had just pricked it; her plum red mouth pouted.

Oh no! It wasn't the shirt—she must have noticed I'd wrecked her project.

"Well, I used your mascara," I tried again. "Debra, you know my eyelashes are nonexistent without it and Mom won't let me have any. . . ."

"That woman is archaic, she only let me shave my legs when I became a werewolf. Really, I detest her sometimes."

What? Debra sympathizing with me? This was not a sister ready to murder me over an art project.

"Listen Liz," my sister is the only one who calls me that, "you keep the mascara, but stay out of my room in the future." Debra changed the subject, quickly. Lady Dracula doesn't stay soft long. "Is this the beast?"

Beauty ran up to Debra the moment she realized she was being talked about. She threw her paws onto Debra's knees. "Watch the tights, doggie," Debra said in a baby tone as she patted Beauty.

Meanwhile I dumped a small amount of puppy chow into Beauty's dish. "SIT!" I commanded as I dragged her over to the food. She wanted to immediately dig in. "NO BEAUTY. SIT!" According to the puppy manual we needed to teach her to wait. I pushed Beauty away from the food and placed my hand on her hindquarters. Down on all fours she dropped. I tugged upwards on her collar and got her into the sitting position. "NOW STAY!" I ordered, holding up my fingers and backing away. She rushed at the food and I pushed her away from the dish again. This stuff had all sounded so easy in the book. "BEAUTY SIT." I forced her into the position again. This time I held her away from the food and counted in my head, *one Saskatchewan, two Saskatchewan, three Saskatchewan* . . . all the way to ten Saskatchewans. "Okay!" I commanded, and released her. She gobbled up the chow in less than five Saskatchewans.

"Well!" Debra commented. "I guess you've found your calling. Animal training."

I shrugged my shoulders. "Debra, can you walk with me to school?"

"What? Am I to protect you from the school bully?"

"No, it's just that I don't want to crate Beauty till Mom wakes up. Beauty can walk with me but maybe you can walk her back."

"Really." Debra's mouth widened a titch, almost a smile. "Sure. I have an easy day today, I just have to hand in my design project."

"Thanks."

"I'm not poopie scooping though."

"Beauty's already gone. I'll bring a baggie just in case."

"Fine. But if she does her business on the way home, I'm making a run for it."

Beauty was supposed to be a family project, but somehow I hadn't pictured Debra ever scooping any dog do.

I left Beauty with her as I quickly used my new mascara. Even my hair behaved smoothly today, lying down flat because of the cool dry weather. I felt great. My sister, tall and in black, walked beside me with her kind of swooping walk. Maybe people watching from their windows might notice a slight similarity between us. Beauty bounded around me, leaping and landing with a happy energy. Dog dancing, it looked like.

I had a tough time keeping up to Debra's swoop, what with Beauty's dancing and my shorter legs, but we did move at a pace. After a couple of blocks we caught up to a familiar figure.

"Hi Elizabeth. Is this your new puppy?" Scott asked me. In the regular daylight, with his baseball cap on backwards, I hardly noticed the disturbing black fuzz growing over Scott's lip.

Is she MY puppy? I felt a quick twinge inside. "No, Beauty is our foster dog," I answered. "We're raising her for the Canine Vision Centre. You know, so she can be trained as a guide dog for blind people."

"Oh yeah, I remember you telling me something about that." Scott kneeled to pat Beauty.

"Don't let her bite you," I told Scott when Beauty nipped at his fingers. "She's not allowed."

Scott pulled his hand away. Beauty licked his face and he smiled, closed his eyes and held up his arms as Beauty continued to lick whatever skin she could find. "Ahh, help!" Scott called. Beauty wagged her tail and jumped on Scott, knocking him over.

"Down Beauty!" I pulled her off him and Scott stood up. He looked at me with his friendly chocolate eyes and grinned. Things were instantly the same between us again. "I think that's really cool, fostering a dog. You going to play Rollerblade hockey tomorrow on the blacktop?"

"Sure." We were close to Centennial Junior High.

Scott moved away from me suddenly and that's when I noticed Alicia rushing up.

"Hi, Elizabeth, where'd you go last night?" Alicia didn't wait for my answer. "Hi Scott," she said softly, as though they shared some secret.

Scott acted differently then. His skin is this olive tone so he never blushes. But his face did something, his skin lightened a shade around his mouth, his eyes shifted around. He walked differently, strutted. Alicia touched his arm as she talked, louder than usual. Her laughter was shriller. They moved ahead of Debra and me, forgetting us completely.

Debra arched one eyebrow, her only comment on the whole scene. I handed her Beauty's leash when we got to the school gate and Debra raised her other hand, spreading her fingers apart in a V. "Live Long and Prosper," she said, her usual Trekker goodbye.

"Thanks Debra. You too. Bye Beauty!"

Beauty hardly glanced at me. She burrowed around in a pile of crumpled brown leaves, wagging her tail. I left the two of them and headed for the school building.

As usual the halls were crowded and kids crashed into me as I headed for my locker. Last year I went to a small elementary school called Mapleview. Except for my red hair, I'm pretty bland and my short body blends into a crowd well. At Mapleview, it never mattered. There were only two grade six classes, I'd gone there since kindergarten, and everyone knew my name and remembered my artistic sister. Now here I was at Centennial, with five hundred kids in grade seven and eight alone. I felt as invisible as my eyelashes when I wasn't feeling awkward and alien.

Someone bumped into me again when I finally stopped at my locker. I took my books out for the morning classes and then just stood there watching in amazement. All those kids swarming the halls, knowing where they belonged and what they were supposed to be doing. They wore their clothes as though they were part of a secret code, and I wasn't sure I used the same code.

Alicia joined me at my locker. "Do you think Scott LIKES me," she asked as she looked in the small rectangular mirror she'd pulled out of her backpack. She smoothed on another layer of wild cherry lip balm and made a face. "Rats. Got some on my teeth." Her tongue swept over them.

"Scott likes everybody," I answered, hoping that was still true.

Chapter 4

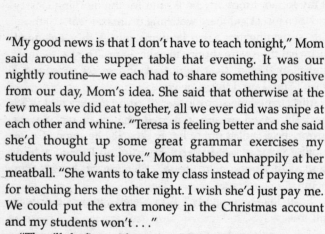

"My good news is that I don't have to teach tonight," Mom said around the supper table that evening. It was our nightly routine—we each had to share something positive from our day, Mom's idea. She said that otherwise at the few meals we did eat together, all we ever did was snipe at each other and whine. "Teresa is feeling better and she said she'd thought up some great grammar exercises my students would just love." Mom stabbed unhappily at her meatball. "She wants to take my class instead of paying me for teaching hers the other night. I wish she'd just pay me. We could put the extra money in the Christmas account and my students won't . . ."

"They'll do fine without you," Dad interrupted.

The edge of Mom's fork suddenly crushed down so hard on a meatball that one half sailed through the air. It landed on the floor and Beauty snatched it up, lightning quick, in her mouth. Just as quickly, Mom leaned over and grabbed Beauty's muzzle. "No Beauty. Give it up." She dug her thumb and forefinger into the corners of Beauty's mouth, forcing her to open it. With her other hand she scooped out the mashed meatball.

"Well, of course they won't enjoy Teresa's teaching

methods as much as yours," Dad quickly added. "Why don't you let the dog have it, Sarah?"

"It's against the rules, Ray. Absolutely no people food for the puppy." Mom wiped the meatball mush off her hand with a dish rag.

"Well, I'm certainly glad you're home tonight. And I'm also really happy Debra is home for a change."

Debra shot Dad one of her Lady Dracula glares. "Whatever does that sweatshirt mean?" She pointed at Dad with her fork.

"My good news for the day," Dad answered.

For the first time I noticed that Dad was wearing a white sweatshirt with bright multicoloured letters.

"DISASTER RECOVERY" Dad read out for us, grinning. "I volunteered for the team. We meet every couple of weeks to discuss strategies and systems start-up procedures in the event of a disaster. Once a year we simulate one."

"I don't get it. You mean you pretend to have injuries and medics treat you?" I couldn't picture this kind of thing happening at Regal Trust.

"No. We just pretend that all the on-site computer systems have shut down. Our back-up tapes are driven every day to another location. On Disaster Day, we have to start up the whole Regal Trust computer system within twenty-four hours. Business as usual for clients the next day."

"So that if there's a fire, earthquake, hurricane or nuclear holocaust, your customers can have an update on their registered retirement savings plan the very next day?" A smirk stretched across Debra's face.

"Something like that." Dad's grin straightened a bit.

"How comforting!"

"It would be, though, don't you think?" I found Dad's news amazing. "Imagine if no matter what happened to you, the very next day you could start over again."

"You can. That's called life," Debra commented.

"It's certainly what life is all about," Mom agreed, "disaster recovery." She turned to Dad. "Aren't you busy enough at work without joining another new project, Ray?"

"It won't be so bad," Dad answered. His grin disappeared altogether.

Everyone chewed and swallowed silently for a while. Then Debra spoke.

"My good news is that I handed in my design project today. I wanted it perfect, so I kept having to redo it from scratch. I couldn't bear to look at it this morning so I just zipped it up into my portfolio and handed it in."

Phew! She hadn't noticed my little mascara stain fix-up. Even Beauty looked relieved.

"That's wonderful, Debra. Isn't it, Ray?"

"Yes, it certainly is." Dad had to be encouraged to comment on this one. He had wanted Debra to go to university. Dad didn't mind if she studied fine arts, or anything really, he just didn't approve of community college diploma programs. "Isn't it satisfying to work hard on something, finish it and turn it in on time?"

"If it's meaningful," Debra answered, her eyes smouldering.

Dad's eyebrows flared. He chewed on a piece of meatball so hard that his jaw and neck muscles rippled. "Meaningful," he said, after he'd swallowed. "Meaningful," he repeated as though tasting the word.

"Sure. For some useless Math assignment or Social Science project, I just couldn't be bothered putting in that much work."

"A board full of D's is meaningful?" Dad asked the rest of his meatballs and spaghetti.

Debra gave Dad another look as black as her clothes. She opened her mouth and then closed it as though it was too much effort to speak.

"We only put two bags of garbage out this week," Mom piped in then. "Our recycling and compost projects are really working."

Nice try Mom, I thought. But now she'd reminded me of something that ticked me off. "Oh yeah! Our newspapers were blowing all over the street on recycling day. It took me half an hour to collect them all up and stuff them back into the Blue Box."

"Well that makes up for you throwing away the peanut butter and Chocotella jars. Didn't think I'd notice, did you?" Mom snapped. "Next week you can tie string around the bundles, Elizabeth."

"Why me? It's always me that takes the compost out too and I don't see any of that wonderful topsoil you said our kitchen scraps would turn into. All we have is a dump crawling with potato bugs."

"Well, it hasn't been long enough. And we need to turn it over. Have you been turning it, Ray?"

"Ah, hmm. I don't think I have, come to think of it."

"And we're supposed to wet it and sprinkle a layer of soil on it from time to time," Mom continued.

"Now that, I'm sure I've never done," Dad commented. "Did you mention all of that before?"

"Several times," Mom answered. She gave Dad her own version of the Lady Dracula glare.

No one bothered talking for a long while. When the fruit salad hit my mouth, Mom finally remembered to ask about the G.A. dance.

"It was okay." I searched my mind for words that wouldn't give away how mixed up I felt about the whole thing, especially Scott and Alicia. "Scott asked me to play Rollerblade hockey tomorrow," I continued, with far too hopeful a tone in my voice. It wasn't something I should have shared with the family—I was just spewing out my thoughts. If he were a completely different person in love with Alicia he wouldn't have asked me to play hockey, would he have? So this to me was good news. But not the way Debra took it.

"Good old Scotty," Debra smirked. "Our little Liz is growing up."

"Oh leave her alone!" Dad growled.

And with that everyone scraped their chairs away from the table and started the supper cleanup. So much for another one of Mom's brilliant ideas.

◆   ◆   ◆

Saturday morning, with helmet, pads and Rollerblades on, I stepped out the door.

"Elizabeth, could you take Beauty with you?" Mom called.

I didn't want to. Not after playing an hour of Stick with the mutt. The score had been Beauty 30, Elizabeth 10. That was tiring enough. Then when I'd taken her into my room so I could finish my Social Studies project on Germany, Beauty had lain quietly underneath my bed. The only trouble was she'd been peacefully chewing up my suede desert boots. They were garbage now, unrecyclable.

"Mom, Beauty's hung around with me all morning. Could I just play hockey by myself?"

"No." Mom held out her list and jabbed her finger at the

paper as she continued: "I have seven loads of laundry to do and I need to wash the floor and vacuum. Unless you want to stay home and . . ."

"What about Dad?"

"He's working on the PC."

"Debra?"

"She's going out with Rolph."

"Aw Mom."

"Beauty needs to socialize with children."

"I'm not a child."

"I didn't mean that. Look, just tie her up when you play hockey. She'll get used to not being able to chase balls and she'll see other kids."

"Fine, could you get her leash? I've already got my Rollerblades on."

Mom attached Beauty for me.

"Come on. Outside Beauty," I said and Mom helped me down the porch stairs.

Beauty scampered ahead of me, innocent and happy. She somehow trapped the leash in her mouth, which was open with all her teeth showing. We made a strange picture, I'm sure, Beauty grinning as she pulled her toy Elizabeth on wheels. I couldn't help grinning too.

Rollerblading along the uneven sidewalk felt as though I was wearing eggbeaters on my feet. I liked the feeling, especially after we occasionally hit a smooth patch of driveway or crossed a street. Beauty must have enjoyed pulling me too because she started to run faster and faster, her hind legs bounding forward over her front paws, her ears waving behind her like flags in the wind.

We were crossing a street when Beauty lost her grin and took on a look of doggie determination. "Slow down!" I started to call but my words were lost in the rush of air. I felt a wheel of my Rollerblade catch in a sewer grate. "Beau—teeee!" I yelled, panicking. But it was too late.

I threw my hands out desperately to break my fall and landed on them and my stomach.

"Ooof." I didn't have any wind left to yell ouch. My wrists hurt from supporting all of my sudden weight and my hands were decorated with tiny pebbles that were drawing blood. "Ow, ow, ow," I repeated when my breath came back. "Beauty, why'd you keep pulling me? Couldn't you see I was stuck?" My hands stung, my eyes watered.

Beauty whimpered and licked at my face. I picked out all the pebbles. Beauty shifted to lick my hands. I wrapped my arms around her neck and buried my face in her fur until my eyes stopped watering. It took a couple of minutes.

"It's okay, Beauty. I'm sorry, it wasn't your fault. Let's just go," I told her softly. She held still and watched as I propped myself up first on one leg and then on the other. I skated off much more slowly. Beauty took the leash back into her mouth, glancing back at me.

As we rolled to the next curb I noticed another sewer grate, and desperately reined Beauty in. "Stop Beauty, wait!" I cried. She caught on just as I was tottering over the edge of the curb. "Go around," I commanded as I directed her with the leash. We made it safely this time.

Scott and two other guys were already playing hockey on the blacktop when I skated in with Beauty.

"Hey, what's with the animal?" Tyler called out to me.

"Hi Elizabeth!" Scott yelled as he wound up a shot and flicked it in the goals under Tyler's legs. "That's her foster dog, Beauty," he answered for me.

"The dog's going in for goals, Tyler. It's gotta do better than you," Alexander ribbed.

"Now that Elizabeth's here, I'm getting out anyway."

Tyler skated forward, leaving the empty net for me.

"Maybe she doesn't want to go in goals yet. She doesn't have to take the first turn," Scott told Tyler.

"You want to be goalie or what?" Tyler growled, turning and facing me.

Well, at least Scott had made Tyler ask me first. But I didn't want Scott having to stand up for me any more than he already had. "Sure. Just let me tie Beauty up." I wound her leash around the bicycle rack and skated over. Only it was hard to brake on Rollerblades, and I ended up knocking over the net.

"I'll be on her team," Scott said, setting the net back up.

"Like always," Tyler sneered.

Like always, I thought and smiled.

"Look out, suckers!" Tyler hollered as he whipped his stick back and connected with the ball, sending it towards me before Scott or I was ready.

"Scott, it's coming for you!" I called.

Scott managed to block the ball at the last minute with his body, making it bounce towards Alexander. Alexander picked it up with his stick, guiding the ball around Scott.

"Gotcha," Scott yelled, hooking the ball away from Alexander as he passed him. The ball rolled loose towards me.

"Got it, Scott," I said and skated easily out from the nets to knock the ball even farther away. Scott and I were playing great defence together as always.

Beauty jumped, barking her cheers.

"All right Elizabeth!" Scott slapped my hand in a high five. Good friends, best friends, using teamwork to keep the ball out of our net. Only two shots made it past us over the next half hour.

Then it was our turn to play offensive. Alexander played

goals and Tyler defence. I passed the ball to Scott and Scott passed it slightly too far ahead of me.

"I've got it," we both yelled. Both of us skated for it. Both of us tried to stop. I tripped for the second time that day, only this time I collided into Scott. He stumbled backwards and caught me in his arms.

Face to face, I noticed the dark hair on his lip again. I also felt his hands on my arms.

"Are you okay?" he asked me softly.

There was something different in his voice. It was as though he was talking to a, a . . . girl, I finally realized. "Fine," I mumbled. A girl is what I am, I thought. Why does that bother me?

"Whoo, whoo, whoo!" Tyler hooted. "Does that feel nice?"

It could have—Scott made me feel special at that moment. But my face suddenly felt incredibly hot.

"Uh-oh. Look out Scott. Here comes your other girl friend," Alexander suddenly warned.

Other girlfriend, that's not the way it was between Scott and me. Good friends, best friends, I repeated to myself and turned to see Alicia coming our way. She was wearing a new leather jacket and her blond hair waved gently in the wind as if she were part of a shampoo commercial.

"Oh hi, Scott," she said as though she had no idea he would be there.

"Hi Alicia," Scott answered a little too loudly. He skated over to her and they started laughing over stupid things. I flicked the ball in past Tyler's foot.

"Great shot," Alexander called.

Scott didn't even notice as he skated off to the side of the blacktop with Alicia. There was no way I could play against both Alexander and Tyler by myself and Tyler didn't want to team up with me against Alexander. I didn't even ask him, so that ended the game.

"I have to go, anyway," I said and skated over to the bicycle rack to untie Beauty. "See you guys later, I have to go," I repeated, shouting this time for Scott's benefit. Still no response.

Tyler started practising shots on Alexander. "See you Elizabeth."

Scott and Alicia finally waved, sort of as an afterthought. I looked at them for a few long seconds, until suddenly Beauty yanked me forward as she bounded off with that silly grin on her face. It took all my concentration not to fall again. "Not so fast, Beauty." She gave me an embarrassed backwards glance, the whites around her caramel-coloured eyes showing.

At the end of the block Marnie and her mom, Mrs. Bond, came into view from another direction. As Marnie walked towards us she bit into a white iced doughnut covered in rainbow-coloured sprinkles. The corners of her mouth were iced and sprinkled too.

"What a cute puppy," Mrs. Bond remarked as they caught up to us.

Marnie bent over and reached out with her doughnut hand to pat Beauty, who licked the icing and sprinkles off Marnie's smiling face. When the doughnut waved in front of Beauty's mouth, she snatched it up.

"NO Beauty!" I tried to pry the remainder of the doughnut from Beauty's jaws. "NO!"

"Doggie likes doughnuts," Marnie said.

"But she's not supposed to take people food," I explained.

"We didn't mind, did we, Marnie?" Mrs. Bond smiled.

"By the way, Elizabeth, would you be free to babysit tonight? Say around seven?"

"Sure."

"Good." Mrs. Bond watched as Marnie slapped at Beauty's body. "Gently now. Maybe Elizabeth will bring the puppy to our house later."

After Beauty had swallowed her last morsel of doughnut, she "hurried up" in front of them.

"Ew!" Marnie said as her nose wrinkled.

"That's enough Marnie. We'd better be going." Mrs. Bond waved goodbye as she dragged Marnie away.

Boy, would I have loved to take off too. Instead I pulled out a plastic bag from my jean pocket. "Good girl, Beauty," I said as I scooped up the doggie do, using the bag as a glove and then turning the bag inside out around it. I couldn't see a garbage pail anywhere. Oh wonderful.

I skated off, and we were far enough away from home that after a while I forgot all about what I was carrying. Swinging the plastic bag back and forth, I bumped into Debra heading out to meet Rolph.

"Surely that isn't what I think it is," Debra said.

"You mean this?" I held up the bag closer to Debra's face, and then explained to her exactly what the contents were.

Chapter 5

Rain started sprinkling down as I headed for the garbage pail in the backyard to dump the Beauty bag. On the clothesline flapped an army of Dad's shirts.

"Hey Mom, it's raining!" I called out when I noticed her back near the compost bin. She was wearing gardening gloves, Dad's rain boots, a big sun hat and a surgical mask. She looked like a beekeeper as she held a hose that pumped water into the bin.

"Mom! Did you hear me? It's raining!"

Mom took off the lid now, peered in with a wrinkled nose, and jabbed a spade into the compost. She mucked around a bit and then finally looked up and noticed me. "Elizabeth, you're back," she said after lowering her mask.

"Yeah. Mom, you want me to take the laundry down so it doesn't get wet?"

"Oh no! It's raining! I thought the drops I felt were from the hose."

I let Beauty loose, walked Rollerblade style to the clothesline—toes down first, arms out for balance—and started taking down the army.

Mom dug at some dirt at the side of the compost bin and shovelled it on top of the compost. She closed up the bin, then sighed and wiped her garden glove across her nose, leaving a dirt smudge behind.

"These'll have to go in the dryer, they're still pretty damp," I told her.

"All that extra work to conserve energy," Mom said. "For nothing."

"Why don't you ever try to save your own energy," I complained when she joined me. She acted as though she hadn't heard me as I unpinned the clothes and handed them to her. We worked together quietly, until I finally had to ask her. "Mom, can men and women just be friends?"

"Just a minute, Elizabeth. Here, let me do that. You go on in. It's starting to really come down."

I didn't care about getting wet. I wanted to know the answer to my question right then and there, but Mom was handling another item on her list.

After waiting a few more seconds, I took Beauty into the house and undid my Rollerblades. The floor felt firm and flat beneath my feet. Mom came in and I followed her down the stairs to the dryer, hoping she would make my life feel solid again to me, as solid as the floor. I tried a different question. "What if you have a friend that's a guy but he's not a boyfriend and a friend that's a girl who wants to be his girlfriend. Does that mean you have to stop being friends with the guy?"

Mom slammed the dryer door and pushed the dial in and around to start it up. "There's nothing wrong with liking Scott, Elizabeth. Don't let your sister tease you."

"But that's not it at all. You haven't been listening!"

"I have been a little busy, Elizabeth. But maybe I understood a different question than the one you actually asked."

"What question?" I didn't understand her at all.

Her back was towards me now as she emptied the next load of laundry from the washer into her basket.

"I don't know, Elizabeth. Can I get back to you on all this later? Maybe after I've had a few moments to myself to think about your question?"

Mom was pencilling me down on her list, I could see it now. "Discuss boy/girl relationships with Elizabeth." She would analyze my problem like one of those short stories she dissected in her English class. But this wasn't what I wanted from her. I needed to hear her tell me, "Of course, Elizabeth. You can be friends with Scott and still be friends with Alicia. Even if she slow dances with him and you feel funny about it. Even if she gushes all over him and takes him away from Rollerblade hockey games." Even with all the time in the world, Mom wasn't going to say that.

I whirled away, hot and angry with her because I knew she couldn't. I walked over to the next room where Dad was sitting in front of the computer. His eyes blinked too quickly, too often, too hard. Like a nervous tick or twitch. He made me angry too. He didn't have an endless list of things like Mom—for him there was always only one thing. "Dad, why do you have to work on a Saturday?"

Dad looked at me, twitch, twitch. "Two people quit in my department and Regal Trust isn't replacing them," he answered. "I have a hundred and twenty man hours of work left on a project and only fifty-five hours to do it in."

I wasn't seriously thinking of asking him about Scott, anyway. You asked Dad questions about hard drives and megabytes, questions with yes, no, or numbers for answers.

Mom came into the room at that moment. She set up her expandable indoor clothesrack and started hanging up socks. "Assign the project to a woman then," Mom snarled.

"Fifty-five woman hours should do it."

Twitch, twitch. Dad focussed back on the computer screen.

I took Beauty Rollerblading the rest of the afternoon to tire her out in case she came along to babysit. Beauty amazed me. When we came to the corner where I had tripped over the sewer grate, she stopped and looked back at me. Then she walked around it. "You're going to make a good guide dog, Beauty," I said, reaching down to pat her. I felt a tightness in my stomach and it surprised me. *I don't love her, she doesn't belong to me*, I thought to myself.

We stopped at Alicia's house so that I could try to get a human to Rollerblade with.

"She's gone to the mall to meet a friend. Funny, I thought that was you," her mom told me. Beauty and I went away alone again.

Shopping isn't my idea of a Saturday thrill anyway, I thought as I rolled away. Crowds of people swarming around too many choices at too many different prices. I never knew what to buy or what to say to the salespeople who hovered as though they thought I was planning to steal something. Lately Alicia seemed to like shopping, though.

Beauty leapt around chasing after her tail. "You wouldn't enjoy the mall, girl, would you, huh? Anyway, you wouldn't be allowed."

♦   ♦   ♦

"My good news," I told everyone that night at supper, "is that Mrs. Bond asked me to babysit Marnie tonight. She wants me to bring Beauty. But I don't know if that's a good idea."

"Of course you should! It's good for her to be around a small child. And besides, I'm going to a reading at Harbourfront tonight."

"I'm tied up with work. Sorry," Dad shrugged.

"Rolph and I are going to a movie."

"Oh fine, so I'm stuck."

"It appears very much that way, Liz."

"Thanks a lot Debra!"

"Girls, girls!" Dad interrupted. "I really want to share my good news. This afternoon I solved the problem on my SOCK 1 abend. Overriding the TRT53 sector didn't help. But when I went to the LINKLIB, I discovered the original code . . ."

"That's great!" I jumped in a little early. Dad's news mostly needed to be translated into humanoid first, and even then it lost something in the translation.

"Too bad it took all of Saturday," Mom commented. "I still can't believe you volunteered for another project. Pretty soon you'll work all Sunday too."

"I have my reasons. Besides, it's 'meaningful' to me."

Using a Debra word like meaningful showed desperation on Dad's part, so I tried to help him out. "It's a great sweatshirt, anyway." He was wearing the Disaster Recovery shirt again. "I really love it," I said, pointing my chicken leg at the lettering.

"Please don't point with your food."

"Sorry, Mom. So what's your good news for today?"

She continued to look grumpy for a moment. Saturday housework catch-up often did that to Mom. "Well, I did get ten things out of ten done on my list so it certainly was a productive day."

"Ten out of ten?" I repeated. "What, do you mark yourself with a red pencil?"

"Certainly not," she huffed. "No one marks with red pencils any more."

Stupid list. And it turned out I wasn't even on it.

◆　　◆　　◆

After supper, I packed my babysitting kit bag with some of my favourite old picture books, my collection of Queenie's Burgers cars, a pad of paper, and my pencil crayons from school. Beauty dragged over her eyeless purple monster. *Stupid dog.* "You better not chew up any shoes while we're there," I warned her. She wagged her tail and dropped the monster near me. "You want me to pack Igor for you?" I threw in some milk bones and some rawhide toys as well.

As it turned out, I didn't have to worry about shoes at all.

When we arrived at the Bond house Marnie's mom began giving me instructions immediately: "Here's the telephone number of where we'll be. Help yourself to the doughnuts on the coffee table in the family room. Eight o'clock is bedtime for Marnie." Mrs. Bond stopped for a second and then continued. "I know it's still a month and a half away, Elizabeth, but are you doing anything Halloween? Mr. Bond will be away on business and I need someone to either take Marnie trick-or-treating or hand out candies."

"I hadn't really thought about it," I told her. No, was what I wanted to say. Halloween is almost my favourite holiday. I love dressing up and getting candy, especially the little bags neighbours prepare and especially if they stick in licorice-flavoured suckers. I didn't think I wanted to be responsible for Marnie when I wanted to be a kid myself that night.

"I understand. Will you let me know?" Mrs. Bond headed out the door. "Bye."

We waved goodbye from the window. Marnie used to cry and scream when her mother left, but then I started bringing my babysitting kit bag.

"What's in there? Can I see now?" she asked, so I dug out a Queenie's Burgers car. It happened to be Mr. Onion Ring.

"You drag it back on the floor, and let it go, watch," I explained to Marnie. Mr. Onion Ring whirled around on his back wheels.

"Woof!" Beauty followed Mr. Onion Ring's movement with her snout, a worried look on her face. When the car did a quick spin about and headed for Beauty, she shifted her paws anxiously and finally scooped the car up in her mouth.

"No! Bring that back!" Beauty ducked underneath a rocking chair, dropped the car and placed her massive paw on top of it.

"Here, let's throw something Beauty's allowed to chase," I suggested to Marnie. I waved a rawhide stick around, distracting Beauty from Mr. Onion Ring, and then handed the stick to Marnie. Marnie pitched it and Beauty bounded after. I snatched up the car from under the rocking chair and threw it in my bag again.

Stick in her mouth, Beauty galloped back to Marnie and actually dropped it in her lap. Marnie patted her with large hard slaps and Beauty in turn lapped at Marnie's face till she fell over giggling.

"Don't Beauty! Don't Marnie!" I said as I saw her draw back to hurtle the stick high in the air. Too late. When the stick came down, it knocked hard against the patio window. "We can't do this inside!" I called to Marnie as I tore after Beauty. Beauty scrambled over the couch in front of the patio window. "Stop Beauty!"

Marnie dashed around the couch, meeting Beauty before I could stop her. "Fetch Beauty," she called, winging the stick down the hardwood floor of the hall this time. Beauty threw herself after it, her nails scratching across the floor as she slid and stumbled.

"Stop Beauty, no!" I made a grab for her as she scrambled past me. Missed! I ran back to head off the game at Marnie's end. Marnie managed one more wild pitch over the other couch. It nicked a lamp, swaying it dangerously, and continued sailing through the air. I caught the lamp before it could fall but the stick landed in the fish tank, sending two waves of water sloshing over the sides.

"Don't you dare, Beauty!"

Too late again, she was already bounding over the couch, sending cushions to the floor. Finally, Beauty leapt onto the chair stationed at the side of the aquarium. Her front paws gripped the edge of the glass as she nosed in the water for her stick.

"Get out of there!" I yelled.

Suddenly Beauty's paws slipped into the water and her snout fell in after.

"Aw Beauty, the fish! Be careful!"

Dripping wet, with the stick in her mouth, Beauty weighed a ton as I finally caught up to her, hoisted her out of the tank and off the chair. I wiped up the water and dried Beauty with Mrs. Bond's paper towels.

The Stick game ended with the score of Beauty 4, Marnie 4, Elizabeth 0 and sidelined due to exhaustion. "I'm never bringing you babysitting again, Beauty!" I hollered at her. She flipped over onto her back and wagged her tail. Her eyes begged me to pat her tummy.

"Help me fix up these cushions, Marnie, and then we're going to colour."

Tail flicking hopefully, Beauty followed behind Marnie as she plunked the cushions back on the couch. I took out my pencil crayons. Beauty licked her lips as though she thought they might be dog treats. "Here," I said to Beauty, tossing her Igor from my kit. She immediately shook the monster around in a noisy mock battle. "Look at me, play with me," her whole body seemed to say.

Luckily without effect this time. Marnie's bottom lip was tucked underneath her front teeth as she concentrated on scribbling big red circles, around and around and around. I worked on a cartoon version of Beauty chewing on the monster.

"Explosions," Marnie announced after finishing. She pointed to some circles, "With fire. There's the fire truck," she explained, pointing to an almost identical set of circles.

"Hmm, I like the colour," I said as I looked over the wild red curves that looked like the tracks of Mr. Onion Ring. Marnie in turn looked over at my version of Beauty.

"Holy, you're the best drawer in the world," Marnie exclaimed.

"No, you have to see my sister draw," I said.

We had our doughnut snack after posting our pictures on the fridge. Boy, Marnie loved doughnuts. There was only one and a half left out of six and I'd eaten only two. I gave Marnie some milk bones to feed Beauty.

"Yum, yum. Doggie likes her snack," Marnie said. "Now we'll feed Freddy, Eddy and Beddy," she announced, heading back for the aquarium waving a half-eaten chocolate dip.

"Not with doughnuts!" I called after her, running to catch up just in case.

"Silly," she told me when I did. "Freddy, Eddy and Beddy eat fish food." Marnie climbed on to the same chair where Beauty had stood earlier and sprinkled a thick layer of food flakes over the surface of the water.

"Careful, Marnie. They can't eat that much, can they?"

I kneeled down in front of the tank, and Beauty sat down beside me. Marnie polished off the chocolate dip as she gazed at the fish tank. There were white rocks lining the bottom and four or five plants with long green leaf fingers waving in the water. A treasure chest opened and closed and a grinning skeleton bobbed out from inside it. I couldn't tell Freddy, Eddy and Beddy apart. Each was your basic goldfish orange, about two thumbs wide with a fantail that doubled its length. They took turns gliding to the top of the water and making large O's with their mouths as they ate the fish food. Beauty sat up tall, eyeing them with her tongue hanging out and her ears partway up, a hopeful look on her face as though she was expecting a Freddy, Eddy, and Beddy snack.

"Come with us, Beauty," I told her as I took Marnie to the bathroom to brush her teeth. "Come on," I coaxed Beauty again as we went to Marnie's bedroom. I was almost sure Beauty wouldn't try her paw at fishing, but not quite.

While I was reading Marnie *The Paper Bag Princess* Beauty fell asleep on her back, paws in the air, tummy up, her whole face smiling in a happy dog dream.

"Aw, doggie's so tired," Marnie said as she looked down.

I couldn't resist patting Beauty's tummy. For someone who ate my best shoes and swam in people's fish tanks as a hobby, she did look really cute. I stayed a while longer with Marnie, and then crept out when she too fell asleep.

The phone warbled, and when I picked it up it was Alicia.

"Hi, Elizabeth. Your dad told me you weren't at home, but I had to guess where you were. He forgot." She paused for a few seconds. "Is he on something?"

"What do you mean?"

"Drugs or something, you know. He sure acted spaced out."

"Dad?" I had to laugh at that one. He's the only person I know who actually bought the "Say No to Drugs" video. "Nah, he's just busy with work."

"Oh well." Another pause. "Listen, we had the most incredible time at the mall."

"We?"

"Vicky and I—and we met Scott at the arcade."

"Oh."

"And we saw some kids play this amazing new game called Virtual Reality. They wore headgear and belts and it was like totally weird."

"Did you try?"

"Nah, we didn't have enough money. But I bought some cool earrings and purple nail polish."

"Purple?"

"Yeah, you can try it. I know how you love purple. Listen, next week is my birthday and Mom wouldn't let me have a party with guys. Feel like coming for a sleepover?"

"Me? Not Vicky?"

"She's coming too, and Lydia and Jessica."

I wanted to be the first and the only one invited, but after a moment I said, "Yeah I'll come. Hold on a sec, I think I hear water running." Slosh, slosh, slosh. I heard the noise faintly but then it stopped. I waited for a moment but it didn't start up again. "Oh well, maybe it was just the pipes. Hey Alicia, what are you going as on Halloween?"

"Halloween? Are you kidding? If I go out at all, I'll throw on some of Dad's old clothes, maybe soap some windows or just hang out."

"Oh."

"C'mon, you weren't planning on getting all decked out and actually, like, trick or treating."

I didn't answer.

"Well, so okay, I'll see you at school."

"Sure. See ya." I hung up the receiver. Alicia wasn't planning on trick or treating, I couldn't believe it. Last year we'd had so much fun. Debra helped us make paper maché dome heads complete with hand-painted purple veins. With sheets dyed glow-in-the-dark green draped over us and those heads on top of our own, we'd gone as aliens. Scott had decorated his yard with gravestones and hid a couple of speakers that played wails and moans when we walked up his path. He dressed up as Frankenstein and scared us out of our wits when he suddenly loomed up on us from the shadows. It had been a bumper crop for licorice suckers too.

Maybe I would take Marnie out on Halloween after all. I sighed, settling back in the family room to watch the rest of the hockey game on TV. A Queenie's Burgers commercial at third period made me grab for the last doughnut in the box. Nothing. I felt around without looking, and then I did look. The box was bare. Not even a crumb or a smear of icing. "Beauty?" I wondered out loud. I heard thumping and looked down to where the sound was coming from. A black tail was wagging against the floor leading from underneath an end table. Sure enough, almost camouflaged in the shadow, Beauty lay licking her lips. The fur on her muzzle was slicked back and wet-looking.

"How'd you get that doughnut?" I asked her. More tail thumping. "Hey Beauty, how did your face get so wet again?" That sloshing noise came back to haunt me. Then something made me look over towards the fish tank. I couldn't see any orange movement. "Oh no! Fred-dy, Ed-dy, Beddy!" I called, not believing I was actually talking to goldfish. I rushed over to the tank, Beauty at my heels. "Tell me you didn't eat them, too, Beauty! C'mon, tell me!"

Chapter 6

"My good news is that Beauty didn't eat Marnie's goldfish." Having pizza for supper on a Sunday night had to be another highlight.

"Surely you know doggies don't eat fish, kitties do," Debra drawled after I'd shared my positive moments with my family at the dinner table. A cheese string hung down the corner of Debra's lips. I watched as she gracefully flicked it into her mouth with her tongue.

"Yeah but Freddy, Eddy and Beddy were totally invisible when I looked over. And I knew Beauty had been in the aquarium. I'd heard the water sloshing and her face was wet," I said, picking off the mushrooms from my slice of pizza.

"A mushroom or two wouldn't kill you, Elizabeth," Mom commented. "Did you give Beauty a bowl of water?" she asked after her next bite. "Maybe Beauty was thirsty and just needed a drink."

"Probably. Especially after that doughnut she scoffed when I wasn't looking," I said. "No, I didn't give her any water. I forgot. But at least the goldfish were alive. They kind of lay there under the plants where I couldn't see them, as if they were sleeping. Do you suppose goldfish sleep?"

"Who could possibly care?" Debra commented.

"They must," my mother said.

"I could call up the library on the modem and check if they have a goldfish book," my father offered.

"Nah, I'll ask Scott at school. He knows everything about fish and aquariums."

"She shouldn't be stealing people food. Beauty's a growing dog. Maybe you should give her a little more puppy chow," Mom concluded.

"You know, if we had a CD-ROM you could look up that information in a flash," Dad continued.

"What information?" I asked.

"About whether goldfish sleep," Dad answered. "Regal Trust is talking about updating their PC's as well as our home systems, so that if they give me a 300 Megabyte hard drive with enough speed, you'll be able to do just that." Dad smiled. "That's my good news for today. I'm sure they'll be giving me one soon."

"Why don't they hire more staff instead of spending money on new systems?" Mom asked.

Dad's grin straightened.

"Will we be able to get any good games for it?" I asked, trying to brighten Dad up again.

"Sure," Dad answered. "And there's all kinds of other things it can do." He glanced at us hopefully, waiting for one of us to ply him for details. No one did.

"The college is adopting a fine paper recycling program—at my suggestion," Mom said, after a suitable pause. "That's what Teresa told me at the reading last night." Her face beamed as though she'd just single-handedly saved the planet.

"Good going, Mom!" I said.

"Rah, rah!" Debra cheered weakly, but she smiled.

"Well, we all have to do our part." Mom's face was pink with pleasure but she didn't wallow long. "So what's your good news today, Debra?"

"Well, I certainly can't top yours." Debra dragged another cheese string into her mouth. "And my goodness, Beauty not eating . . . what were their names again?"

"Freddy, Beddy and Eddy."

"That's right. Beauty not eating those goldfish—I have no life compared to Elizabeth. As far as Dad's news, a CD-ROM PC with more megabytes, that could be the very thing that saves this family."

"Come up with something," Mom said, "that's the rule. Even if you only saw a lovely sunset."

"A sunset. No, didn't see one of those. Hmm. I know! My graphic arts teacher told us he was handing our design projects back tomorrow." Debra glows when she's happy, just like Mom. And at that moment we could have used sunglasses to look towards Debra's or Mom's side of the table.

"You're that sure you got a good grade, eh?" Dad asked.

"I must have. It was perfect. College is so much better than high school. And I'm finally doing something I'm really good at. I can't wait to get my project back."

"That *is* good news, then." Mom patted Debra's arm.

Dead, I'm as good as dead, I thought.

"I'll be happy too as long as you can get a job later," Dad concluded.

The two Lady Draculas glared at him.

"You can always get a degree and then teach art," Dad offered, backing away from an argument. That line still didn't soften the glare so he spoke more quickly. "But I really am glad about you working so hard on that project. That's really great news."

"Does anybody have any good ideas for a Halloween costume?" I asked before anyone could jump on him.

"Halloween? You're almost thirteen. You can't mean you're going trick-or-treating again," Debra said.

"I have to take Marnie next door. It's more like a babysitting job. But I still want to dress up, keep in the spirit, you know."

"Hmm. It's not exactly Halloween tradition, but the What store has reindeer antlers if you want to go as Rudolph. They're supposed to be for pets but I suppose the size must be adjustable," Debra offered.

"Why don't you ever wear the same costume twice? Or trade with your friends," Mom suggested. "If you dressed as a reindeer, we have the Peter Pan costume you needed for your grade two play somewhere. Marnie's mom could make some adjustments and Marnie could be an elf."

"You just gave me an even better idea! Dad, do you still have your Santa Claus costume from the Regal Trust Christmas party?"

"They store it at work, but I can get it."

"I'll go as Santa Claus, Marnie can be the elf and Beauty can be Rudolph."

Beauty's ears perked up when she heard her name and she gave a sharp bark.

"Quiet Beauty," Mom commanded.

Beauty whined a soft apology and laid her head down between her paws. I wondered to myself how I could make her nose glow. Details, I thought. It didn't matter. Neither Debra or Alicia could make me feel stupid about trick-or-treating while I was babysitting, and with this great Santa Claus idea I could really look forward to Halloween now. Alicia, birthday—that's how my mind moved ahead to my next problem.

~ 53 ~

Alicia and I seemed to be on different time paths now. She had fast-forwarded into near adulthood while I was on pause frame in childhood. What could I get her that wasn't too babyish?

Since Debra was in a rare mood and full of good ideas always, I thought I'd ask her. "Alicia's invited me to her sleepover this weekend. It's her thirteenth birthday."

"Really, Liz. That's almost more exciting than your goldfish story."

"Yeah, well, thirteen seems so much older than twelve. I don't know what to get her. Debra, you're more sophisticated, maybe you could come up with something?" I thought flattery was my best approach. It worked.

"Rolph and I want to go to the mall tomorrow anyway. There's a discount on the Virtual Reality video game Mondays and Rolph wants to check out the graphics. You could meet us there after school," Debra suggested.

"Thanks! I will. At the Cyberforce Arcade?" I asked.

"Four o'clock sharp. You're late, we're gone."

♦   ♦   ♦

I knew better than to be late for an appointment with Debra anyway, so I ran to the bus right when the bell rang at 3:00. I got off at Fairview Mall by 3:20 so I scouted ahead for possible birthday presents. I browsed in a bookstore, but Alicia reads books that all look alike and go by numbers instead of titles. I didn't know what numbers she'd read. Besides, her thirteenth birthday was a landmark and needed something more special to mark it than a *Happy Valley #37* or a *Terror Cliff #83*. I checked out the What store right across from the Cyberforce video arcade and picked up Beauty's Halloween antlers. There were lots of bizarre glow-in-the-dark T-shirts, and I wanted to buy Alicia one that read "I'm too sexy for this shirt" but I didn't have enough money.

Rolph and Debra walked into the arcade as I paid for Beauty's antlers, so I crossed over to them. "Hi Rolph," I said.

"Hello, little sister," he answered, smiling. Rolph looked overly ordinary for an arts student, animation yet. His hair was short and bushy blond, his body was thick and he had a sharp nose and controlling grey eyes. He was wearing black jeans, Debra's touch probably, and a white shirt with a tiny cow embroidered on his pocket—the only whimsical thing about him.

"Hi Debra."

"You're early. How much money do you have to spend on Alicia?" she asked.

"Eight dollars."

"That will certainly limit your choices. Come on. Watch us play the game."

The arcade was a black tunnel lit up by games on both walls as well as the aisle down the centre. In a fenced-off section along the left wall were two glossy black pods facing each other like the cockpits of rival spaceships. "VIRTUAL REALITY" the sign above them read, and a smaller one across the divider fence warned "Please do not touch, this equipment is expensive." Two spectator monitors hung from the ceiling showing the graphics from each player's viewpoint. They looked stark and eerie. Suspended in space was a large square with red and white checked tiles connected by stairs to four other elevated squares with blue and white tiles. There were mustard-coloured pillars and white archways on all levels of the complex. Occasionally, a grey geometric shape whirled by, a meteorite I guessed, and less occasionally, a big green prehistoric bird flew across the screen.

"It's supposed to be as though you're really in the game in another dimension," Rolph explained to Debra and me.

"For five bucks a ticket, it should be," I said.

"It's an exceptional experience." Debra gave me her Lady Dracula stare.

"An exceptional experience," I repeated. "That's it! I'll buy a ticket for Alicia's birthday present."

"Good thinking, little sister," Rolph said. "The Monday special is four tickets for fifteen dollars. We'll split the cost. Seven-fifty each."

Somehow I distrusted Rolph's economizing skills. Artists weren't supposed to be good with money, were they? We strode over to the counter and paid for our tickets.

"Read these directions, please," the attendant instructed. He pointed to a poster on the wall:

> **Virtual Reality—a leap into the future. The attendant will strap you in, secure the helmet on your head, and hand you the joystick. The thumb button will walk you forward and the index finger button will fire missiles at your opponent. A pterodactyl may attack at any time, so look to the sky when you hear the screeching. Good luck.**

"All clear?" the attendant asked.

Rolph nodded curtly. Debra looked blank-eyed and nervous. Another attendant led her to her pod.

I watched as he fastened a belt around her waist and loaded her down with the special helmet. Black and cumbersome, it seemed like something a deep sea diver or space robot might wear.

"It's so heavy," Debra complained as she held her head with both hands.

The attendant stepped back. "Here, let me adjust that for you. Can you see okay?"

Debra tried to nod, looking like an interplanetary visitor from Star Trek.

"There are television cameras built in so that you'll actually feel as though you're walking in the direction that you aim your body towards."

"Uh huh." Words were failing Debra for once. She gripped at the visor as if it were a blindfold.

"All right. Practise walking around."

Debra became a yellow-haired little man in a blue jumpsuit on one of the two monitors attached to the ceiling. The video man's legs pumped quickly for a moment as the figure scurried frantically across the platform.

"Not so fast," the attendant told her. The little figure's legs moved more calmly. "That's it. Tell me when you have the feel of it."

Rolph looked thicker and more powerful with the helmet on. With his feet planted apart and the joystick at arm's length from his body, he became a Borg or some other dangerous space invader. His video man, identical to Debra's except that he was wearing a red jumpsuit, strutted calmly across the screen. "Ready," Rolph called out.

"Okay. Now remember, you can communicate to each other just by talking normally. There's a link between the two helmets. Ready. Go!"

I stood behind the fence trying to watch both monitors. One showed Debra's video man, the other Rolph's. I could see both figures moving towards each other. Debra never stood a chance. Rolph's red-suited man crept around behind her. "Up near the pillar, Debra," his voice boomed over the arcade loudspeakers.

The pillar was in another direction. Debra whirled towards it like a frightened child playing blind man's bluff. Rolph was really on the opposite side.

Debra's sharp intake of breath hissed over the speakers.

As Rolph raised his joystick higher, I could see parts of his arm and the gun through his monitor. "Take that," Rolph called as he pressed the red button. Two shots missed, then a direct hit!

"Rolph? Rolph? Rolph!" Debra cried out in a perplexed voice. On the monitor showing Rolph's view, Debra's graphic body exploded into bits. One to zero for Rolph.

She rematerialized after a few moments and ran up the stairs away from Rolph.

"Watch out for the bird, love," Rolph told her. I couldn't see any pterodactyl on the screen but Rolph's warning made Debra look up.

"Where, where?" she asked. Meanwhile Rolph was sneaking up behind her.

"Look behind you," I warned, too late.

Rolph blew Debra up.

"Oh come on, Rolph," Debra complained.

"There's the bird again," he called when Debra's body reappeared. She wouldn't fall for the same trick twice. Unfortunately Rolph counted on this reaction.

I could hear the pterodactyl shrieking and flapping its wings. "The bird's really there this time," I called but I don't think she could hear me. As she continued to face Rolph and raise her joystick to blast him out of reality, the pterodactyl picked her up.

"Oh shoot," she snapped. Or maybe she said something a little stronger. Her monitor showed an aerial view that spun around when the bird finally dropped her. Then Debra opened fire, four white puffs leaving her gun. Rolph was back on the square from where the pterodactyl had snatched her. "Rolph, I hate this, where are you?"

"Over here. Come on!"

The tiny mechanical Debra scuttled up some stairs across a platform and around a pillar. No Rolph. Back down the stairs she went, and across a different platform.

"Well, well, we meet again," Rolph said when the two figures faced each other.

Agonizingly slow, Debra fired once, twice, and then finally on the third try, success. "Yess!" she called out jubilantly as bits of the graphic Rolph flew across the monitor.

I couldn't help jumping up and down too. But her victory lasted for only a few seconds.

Then Rolph rematerialized and rushed to Debra's platform, his gun already aimed for her. "Hello love, I'm back from the grave," he whispered, and blew her up again.

None of Rolph's shots ever went wild. He was a deadly accurate marksman and a persistent stalker. Six more times he hunted Debra down. In the three and a half minutes of the game, Rolph obliterated my sister nine times to her one lucky shot.

"Don't worry, Debra. Good heavens, it's only a game," Rolph's voice consoled Debra over the speaker system. He sauntered out of the pod with a smile on his face.

Debra's face seemed chalkier than usual when the attendant lifted the helmet off her. "Grab the pod to steady yourself," he told Debra, taking her hand and placing it on the black padded enclosure.

"How did you like it?" the other attendant asked Rolph.

"The graphics could have been better. Although blowing up my girlfriend was exhilarating."

I'd never liked Rolph before, but in that moment I hated him.

Chapter 7

As soon as we walked in the door Beauty threw herself at me, wagging her whole body.

"The beast really likes little sister," Rolph commented. *He* had came home with us for supper.

"Her name is Beauty," I snapped. "And my name is Elizabeth!" I stalked out the back with Beauty, not bothering to hitch her to the leash.

I broke into a run, around and around the yard, letting off steam and exercising Beauty. She bounded after me with her mouth open in a grin and her tongue hanging out. Her eyes drank in every move I made with a kind of worship. What had I ever done to earn that? It made me feel uncomfortable in one part of my brain, but mostly it made me feel good. When I stopped to catch my breath, Beauty sat down close beside me.

I bent over to pat her and she brushed her paw against my leg. Was Beauty patting me back? Cute. I reached under her head to scratch her chin and she lifted her paw onto my hand. "Friends?" I asked her gently and shook it. Beauty slobbered all over my face and then broke away as though she was embarrassed showing me this much affection. She jogged back with a stick in her mouth.

"Give it," I told her, holding out my hand. She dropped it at my feet, sat down and put her paw in my hand again.

"Friends?" I repeated and shook Beauty's paw. "All right!" I called out loudly, realizing that Beauty had remembered the trick. I tried again after a few more stick throws. "Friends," I said, holding out my hand. Sure enough she plunked her paw into my hand.

"She shook hands three times," I told everyone as I stabbed at my pork chop. "It was the most amazing thing. Every time I held out my hand, she gave me her paw. And she taught herself to do it."

Mom dropped her fork full of peas. "Did you get her to go to the bathroom while you were out there?"

I lay down my knife. "Uh no, I forgot. Why?"

"Beauty didn't," Mom said, pointing to a puddle in the corner. Beauty, meanwhile, slept innocently curled up in her crate.

I stood up and hunted through Mom's broom cupboard for something to clean up Beauty's accident.

"Oh let me," my mother said, breathing exasperation hotly into every word. She took out a bag of rags from the same cupboard, flung one out on the puddle and wiped it up. Afterwards she damp-mopped over the corner. One of Beauty's eyes batted open as she watched Mom's mop, then it quickly shut as Mom headed for her. "I guess I'll feed her later when she wakes."

"Sit down and feed yourself," Dad encouraged. "Before everything gets cold."

Mom continued shuttling back and forth between the fridge and the table with more condiments. Applesauce, butter, milk—finally she sat down with a big breath. "So Debra," she began immediately. "Your father and I can't wait to hear your good news tonight."

"We can't?" Dad asked, spooning sour cream on his baked potato.

Mom glared.

"We can't," Dad repeated, still looking for clues from Mom.

"You remember, Ray, the design project."

"Design project, yeessss." Dad's brain powered up like a very slow computer. "I am anxious to hear your good news."

Debra glanced over to Rolph hesitantly. He put his hand over hers, solidly, with a sense of ownership.

"Actually, I'd like to tell you about Rolph's good news." Debra directed her words at Dad. "Rolph sent out an inquiry to Disneyland for work and today he got a positive response. I just thought you'd like to hear that, seeing as you're so worried about work in the field of art."

"Jobs in general, actually. But that is comforting to hear. Disneyland, eh?" Dad chewed his mouthful of potato enthusiastically.

In California, I thought. *Good, the farther, the better.*

"Yes sir. I sent my résumé and slides of my work and they said they wanted me to contact them when I graduated. For a possible interview."

Dad nodded silently.

"But what about *your* good news, Debra," Mom interrupted. "Come on, we all want to know how you did on your graphics project."

"S," Debra hissed.

"S?" Dad echoed. "What do you mean, S?"

"I mean the grade I received on my graphics project was S." Debra enunciated every word as though she were explaining to someone from another planet.

"What does this S stand for? Superior? Superlative?"

"Satisfactory," Debra answered in an even monotone, but her knife screeched across her plate as she cut her porkchop.

Everyone stopped eating for a moment.

"Did your teacher tell you if you did anything wrong, I mean, if you smudged a D or something?" I asked.

"Just drop it, Liz." Debra's voice crackled like static.

"Debra?" my mother questioned.

Debra gave up pretending not to care about her grade. Her hand grabbed at her forehead and then pushed back her hair. "I thought I was so good at art and with all that work . . . ." Debra's voice continued on the edge of breaking down. "I probably should have gone into something boring and simple. Business Computers."

"Well, I'll just go into that college and see your instructor . . . what's his name?" Dad huffed.

"No!" Debra shouted. "You can't help!" With that she scraped back her chair and ran out of the room. We al¹ heard her stomp up the stairs and then slam her dooɪ violently.

There was an uncomfortable silence while everyone stared at Rolph.

He smiled. "Debra really is talented," he explained. "But it is hard to be surrounded by a whole classroom of similarly talented people." I couldn't believe him. He just continued eating. "Actually there are only three grades: S+ being the most desired, S for satisfactory as Debra told you, and S-. Really S is a respectable first-time grade."

"Poor Debra. Those D's were beautiful, perfect in every way. How could she possibly have improved upon that project?" Mom asked.

The mascara cover-up, the tiny little darker dab of paint on the downstroke of one of her D's. I was convinced I had caused

Debra to lose the plus in her grade.

Rolph shrugged his shoulders. "Would you kindly pass the potatoes, Elizabeth?"

I threw one at him but he caught it and winked at me.

"Debra needs to work this out on her own. As an artist, she must toughen herself to rejection. And as I said S is a satisfactory grade." Chomp, chomp, chomp.

Rolph liked watching Debra being blown to smithereens, I thought, in more ways than one.

Later on I heard the soft murmur of voices coming from Debra's room. The rule was, when Debra entertained a guy in her room she had to keep the door open. So when I walked by on the way to the bathroom and heard these strange "Mmm, mmm, mmm," noises, I couldn't help stopping and staring. What I saw froze me to the spot.

Rolph and Debra were pawing each other and kissing in a disgusting, open-mouthed way.

Two thoughts collided in my mind at that moment. *How can she do that with him?* and *I'll never ever do that with anyone.*

Chapter 8

"Did he kiss you?"

Alicia lay on her bed in the centre of the room. Her freshly purple-painted nails now matched the shade of her duvet and wallpaper—that is, the part that showed in between the baskets of kitten pattern. It was one of our favourite jokes that Alicia was a cat person while I, of course, was a dog fan. She waved her fingers in the air to dry them. Cotton wads wedged apart her toes, which were also sticky with the last coat of Loving Lavender Nail Gloss. Alicia didn't answer, but she smiled.

"Well?" Vicky sat cross-legged at the top of the bed, watching Alicia.

The other girls at the sleepover, Jessica and Lydia, sprawled on air mattresses at the opposite side of the room. They seemed to be totally absorbed in coating their nails—as though they weren't really waiting for Alicia's answer, but I knew they were. It was all they ever talked about: guys, kissing, makeup, and clothes.

I was waiting too, hoping for a different answer than everyone else. Sitting on a flip-out chair by myself in a corner, third layer of polish already dried, I focussed on Alicia's desk. It was white, with two drawers on the right-hand side and a hutch attached to the top with a ledge for a computer monitor—only instead the ledge held a portable television topped with two cat figurines. I stared hard at the small screen till I thought I saw Debra and Rolph on it pawing each other and making that disgusting "mmm, mmm" noise.

"C'mon, did he kiss you or not?" Vicky repeated.

I didn't hear Alicia say anything but she probably nodded yes because suddenly Jessica and Lydia gave up their pretence and congratulated Alicia as though she had just announced her engagement.

"Aw he's so cute. You're so lucky!"

The picture on the dark TV screen turned into Scott and Alicia. "What was it like?" I couldn't believe I'd asked that.

Everyone stopped and stared at me.

"Hmm. Gentle, soft, melting. I can't describe it." Alicia sighed. Jessica, Vicky and Lydia heaved big breaths of romantic sympathy.

I felt like throwing up.

"Pizza's here, girls," Alicia's mom called, interrupting the hot air session. Alicia doesn't eat in her room so we all followed her down the stairs and into the kitchen. Mrs. Jackson hung around with a camcorder in her hand, which cut down on our conversation, especially on the subject of kissing. She pointed it at us while we ate our pizza.

I concentrated hard on taking small bites and keeping my mouth closed as I chewed so that I wouldn't look too stupid on the video.

"Mom, could you give it a rest, puh-lease?" Alicia begged after about a minute.

"All right. Just let me get you making your own sundaes and I'll disappear."

Quietly everyone scooped out their favourite flavours of

ice cream. There were three different sauces, and Alicia and I accidentally grabbed for the hot fudge sauce at the same time. Alicia pretended to struggle with me.

"Don't worry, I'll leave you some," she snickered after winning out. She raised the container high and poured the sauce for an extra long time.

"Want some whipped cream?" Lydia asked, shaking the can near Alicia's head.

"Nah, that would just spoil the effect."

"How about you, Elizabeth?" The can pointed at me now.

"No thank you."

SSSSSH! The cream squirted out all over my face. "Whoops, sorry, this can has a mind of its own."

"Yeah, right!" I snapped at her, wiping the drooping gob off.

Vicky and Jessica cracked up. Alicia joined them. If only I could have just laughed along with them.

"Mad can strikes again," Lydia said, this time aiming at Jessica. SSSSSH!

"Eeek!" A fluffy white moustache streamed down Jessica's cheeks now. She wiped it into her mouth with one finger. "Delicious!"

"Oh really?" Alicia snatched the can from Lydia's hands. "I think *Lydia* should have some then!" She shook the can, turned it upside down and sprayed the cream all over Lydia's face.

"Girls! My floor," Alicia's mom called, but she didn't stop the camcorder for one moment.

Whipped cream drooped down from Lydia's eyes, nose and mouth. Breaking up into giggles, Alicia was no match for Vicky when she snatched for the can. Vicky quickly lathered her face with a whipped cream beard.

"Here, have some sprinkles." Lydia gently pitched some on Alicia's beard.

Mrs. Jackson was laughing now too.

"No sauce, please, no sauce!" Lydia raised her arms in front of her head when Jessica came towards her. She collapsed, shrieking and snorting. Everyone was in on the fun except me.

After things had died down and we'd cleaned up, Mrs. Jackson played the video on the TV. Over and over, backwards and in pause frame, we watched the whipped cream food fight. Each time I sounded crabbier and looked more out of it.

Finally Alicia moved on to opening presents. She unwrapped three pairs of dangly cat earrings, two boxes of bath beads, and one Scratch and Smell T-shirt.

"These earrings are just so cute," Vicky commented.

"I've got a T-shirt like this one. I wear it all the time," Jessica said.

"I love bath beads, don't you?" Alicia asked.

"You haven't opened my present yet," I interrupted. Even though I'd drawn thirteen coloured balloons on the envelope, it just lay there flat and easy to overlook.

"I don't see any other presents. Where is it, Elizabeth?"

"Here." Finally I just picked up the envelope and handed it to Alicia.

"Oh there! Thanks Elizabeth."

I watched her face as she carefully untucked the envelope. Her brows knit as she read the words across one ticket certificate.

If she didn't like my present, I knew we couldn't be friends any more. It was tough enough with her taking Scott away from me . . . and all these new friends.

Suddenly her brows smoothed out and upwards in

~ 69 ~

happy surprise. She broke into a grin. "All right! Two tickets for Virtual Reality. You're the best, Elizabeth."

For a moment I felt as though I was again—the best, or at least her best friend. So what if I didn't fit in with these new girls. I licked at some dried whipping cream just above the corner of my mouth.

Vicky ended the moment with her singsong taunt. "Bet I know who you're taking to the arcade."

Alicia didn't say anything, but she blushed, which was worse. I had bought the tickets for her to use with whomever she wanted. But somewhere deep down inside I must have hoped, maybe even expected her to ask me.

"You're all too young to be so boy crazy," Alicia's mom called from the sink.

"C'mon, let's go back to my room," Alicia suggested, making pointed eye signals towards her mother and still blushing.

One of us was too young, anyway.

We trooped back to Alicia's bedroom. Everyone sprawled out in the same spots as before.

"What should we do now?" Lydia asked after a few minutes of talking about nothing.

"I know. Why don't we try to contact Old Man Huntington on the Ouija board?" Jessica said. Huntington had been the principal of Mapleview Elementary about ten years ago. He'd died of a heart attack after a fundraising run around the school. Before he died, he'd chewed someone out for tripping one of the kindergarten kids. No one knew if he'd died because of the running or the yelling or whether it was just one of those things. A few students who stayed late one night rehearsing for a play claimed they heard running footsteps and someone moaning and wailing NO RUNNING IN THE HALL. The someone was presumed to be Huntington.

"Sure," Alicia answered, bouncing from her bed. She pulled open the drawer underneath it and I noticed a pile of *Seventeen* magazines stacked inside. Geez. She used to keep her old Lego collection in there. Alicia pulled out the Ouija box from next to the magazine pile.

"Wait, we need a candle," she said and dashed from the room.

"Get the lights," Vicky ordered after Alicia returned with a lone white candle.

Jessica flipped the switch. The room blackened to leave an eerie flickering spotlight around five pairs of hands all squeezed in, lightly fingering the black plastic triangle.

"Is the spirit of Old Man Huntington present?" Alicia asked.

The triangle glided quickly and smoothly as though it had a life of its own. The sharpest angle paused, pointing to the T and then H A T S M R H U N T I N G T O N T O Y O U.

We looked at each other and snickered. Although it sounded like something a principal might say, I had a feeling Vicky was directing the Ouija.

"What should we ask him?"

Vicky smiled. "Does Alicia have a secret admirer?" she asked.

The triangle slid quickly over to the No.

"He's not a secret admirer, dummy," Lydia said.

"Oh, all right. Who loves Alicia?"

I wasn't so sure it was Vicky moving the Ouija any more. Maybe it was Lydia. The Ouija spelled out S C O T T slowly but surely.

"Oh yeah," Vicky broke in. "What about Elizabeth. Does she have a secret admirer?"

The triangle didn't move for a long time. Then sharply it yanked over to YES. I started to think this wasn't fun any more. It felt creepy. My body felt cold.

"Who is the admirer, Mr. Huntington?" Vicky asked.

The triangle moved first slowly, hesitantly, then sharply in large jerks. B . . . E . . . A . . . U . . .

"I'm not playing this any more. This is stupid," I said, throwing my hands up in the air and stopping the Ouija before it could add the last two letters. Everyone scrambled into their sleeping bags then. Jessica told some stupid knock knock jokes. Vicky talked about a guy she liked named Todd. Lydia complained about her parents. I said nothing, pretending to doze off.

Who'd moved the Ouija around to spell Beauty? Only Alicia knew about Beauty. She must have done it. Was she making fun of me? The only admirer I have is a dog. I only fit in with animals. My only friend is Beauty. While the other girls chatted and giggled, I dozed off thinking those thoughts.

Chapter 9

The next morning I was the first one up.

"Cereal or waffles?" Alicia's mom asked.

I glanced at the double row of miniature cereal boxes in front of me—the variety pack. Mom would never buy something so overpackaged, which made it that much more appealing. "Cereal, please." I smiled. Ripping off the outer cellophane from the boxes, I chose Sugar Flakes, a brand Mom would also never buy, even in the jumbo economy size. I pressed my spoon across the hyphenated line in the middle of the cereal box.

"Better use these," Mrs. Jackson suggested, handing me the scissors. "You can use a bowl, you know."

"I want to see if this works," I said, cutting through the perforation. "You're supposed to be able to put the milk right into the box." I poured some in. So you waste some packaging but you save yourself washing a bowl. It made sense to me.

Alicia joined me then. "Waffles please," she answered her mom, and Mrs. Jackson slid some down in the toaster. "Why are you eating from the box?" she asked me.

"I like it better this way," I scowled. By now there was a milky film seeping through the box onto the table. If I didn't eat quickly, I'd need to use a bowl.

"Trust you!" she said and poured syrup over her toasted waffle.

"Would you like a waffle too, Elizabeth?" Mrs. Jackson asked. "Oh dear, your box is leaking, here!" She handed me a wad of paper towels and a bowl.

It wasn't working. I started feeling guilty, wiping up the puddle, thinking of Mom and her beaming face when she'd told us about the fine paper recycling project at the college. "Yes, I would love a waffle too, please," I said and then cringed as Mrs. Jackson tore into another package of precooked frozen toaster waffles. By the time my waffle popped, Vicky had straggled in from the bathroom looking grey and half-asleep.

"So you want to go to the mall?" Alicia asked me as she wiped her mouth with a paper serviette. How many trees did Mom say it took to make a package of serviettes or a roll of paper towels?

"Maybe." I felt a layer of sugar coat my teeth as I ate my syrup-soaked waffle.

"We could check out the arcade," Alicia suggested.

Maybe she would use one of the Virtual Reality tickets on me after all. I hesitated, wiping my mouth with the death of another tree.

"You think Todd and Scott will be there?" Vicky asked, her face suddenly brightening.

Of course. And I'd have to stand and watch them play the game together. The sugar on my teeth became sickeningly sweet. I suddenly needed to escape the house of environmental disaster. "You know, on second thought, I better go. I have to walk the dog." I didn't mention Beauty by name. My secret admirer, according to the Ouija, my one true friend.

"Do you have to go right this minute?" Mrs. Jackson said, grabbing the empty glass syrup bottle and pitching it in the garbage.

Where's their recycling box? I thought, searching the corners of the kitchen. I didn't see it. "Yes, I really think I need to go right now."

"Well, so okay, like call me later when you're not so busy," Alicia said as she watched me roll my pillow in my sleeping bag.

I threw on my coat and slid my feet into my duck boots. "Oh sure, later," I said and waved the finger that wasn't tied up in the handle of my kit bag.

A gust of wind whipped my hair against my face as I closed the door behind me. It whistled in a worried moan and made the bare tree tops sway and creak. Cold, cold, I hate the cold and it was only the beginning of October too. I ran in short bursts, trying to escape it quickly. Dead, rust-coloured leaves and bits of paper blew in a whirlwind against the curb. One more quick run and I was home.

"Hello!" I called as I slammed the door and kicked off my boots.

A series of yips, yaps and howls ending in a bark greeted me. I walked into the kitchen and glanced over to Beauty's crate. Beauty threw herself at the door. What were those white lumps in her fur? At the back of the crate lay Igor in pieces—a purple body in one corner, an eyeless head in the other, the arms and legs pointing helplessly towards Beauty's water dish. The white lumps were bits of stuffing.

"Doggie missed Elizabeth," my sister drawled at me from the kitchen table.

"Why don't you call her by her real name?" I snapped. I opened the crate door and Beauty leaped out onto me as I crouched down to pat her.

"Ooooh, sleepovers make for testy tots," Debra commented.

"Calm down," I told Beauty as she knocked into my chin with her head. She seemed desperate to paw and lick every square inch of me. "Easy girl." I tried to push her off gently. She lapped at me even more frantically. "Did anybody take Beauty for a walk last night?"

"Mom and Dad went to a play at the college, and to tell you the truth, Rolph and I found better things to do."

"I bet," I answered. "Did you find the time to play a few games of fetch with her?" I kept patting Beauty and trying to dodge her tongue.

"Rolph may have when he took her out for tinkles. But it's you she loves, Liz."

"Shut up, Debra." Beauty, my secret admirer, my temporary dog, she couldn't love me. I took the bag of puppy chow out of the kitchen cabinet. "Sit, Beauty!" I raised up a warning finger. Beauty looked as though she wanted to argue, lifting her muzzle in the air towards me and opening and closing her mouth, but finally she lowered her haunches.

I poured the chow into her dish. "Stay!" I warned and then released her with a nod and the command "Okay."

Beauty raised herself, ambled forward and started into the food.

"She's getting good at that," Debra offered.

"It didn't even take long. She's amazing," I agreed.

"You should sew her toy back together. Beauty didn't mean to tear it apart."

I shut one eye and looked at Debra. She knew I hated sewing. In Family Studies I stitched the pocket of my apron project to the wrong side and hemmed the bottom edge to my jean leg. Six out of ten the teacher gave me on that project, only because she felt sorry for me, I'm sure.

Still, I didn't like to see Igor all in pieces like that. Beauty's favourite toy was my favourite stuffed animal too. And it was a souvenir of Scott, the Scott before Alicia that is. I removed thread and a needle from Mom's junk drawer. "Don't you come near me!" I warned Beauty as I attempted to force a frayed end of white thread through the eye of the needle. Beauty jostled me just as one piece of fray passed through. "Beauty, stop!"

"Oh here, let me." Debra deftly threaded the needle and then proceeded to repair Igor.

◆　　　◆　　　◆

On Monday afternoon Dad walked in the house carrying a large brown box.

"Dad you're home early!" I rushed over to him. "And you remembered the Santa Claus suit!"

"WOOF!" Even Beauty found this unusual.

No clunk of his briefcase. His whole body sank into the couch in a sigh, the box landing on his lap. Beauty sat on top of his feet, wagging small vigorous wags as she waited for a reassuring pat.

"Can I see?" I lifted up Dad's hands and he didn't protest or resist. I raised the lid and looked inside. Junk. A couple of coffee mugs, three framed photographs, a day calendar, a name plate, a Best Year End Ever 1992 trophy. "Dad, what is this?" Beauty stood up and nosed my hands for a treat.

"Eighteen years," Dad answered. He stared into some imaginary screen, not twitching, not blinking, nothing. It was scary.

The front door banged as Mom came in.

"Mom, Mom. Come quick. Dad's acting weird." Well weirder than usual.

"You're home, Ray." Mom noticed the contents of the box. "Oh no!"

"I got called into Cutter's office. Regal Trust is downsizing."

"Downsizing?" I repeated.

"That's when a big company fires people to save money," Mom explained.

"Isn't that a hoot. Regal Trust thinks they need the money more than we do." Dad snorted and shook his head with disgust.

"Dad's fired?"

"Ray?"

"Fired, laid off, whatever you want to call it."

"But how can they do that to you, Dad?"

"Well they give me job counselling services and eighteen months severance pay. We should try and think of it as a nice long vacation, heh, heh." Dad's laugh was more like a cough.

Mom threw herself on the couch beside Dad. "How could they, oh Ray." She leaned her head to his and wrapped an arm around him.

"A security guard escorted me out of the building."

"Oh, oh, oh. It doesn't matter."

I sunk down on the other side of the couch. Now Beauty shifted her attention back to me, laying her head on my lap. I patted her softly. *Poor Dad!* With my free arm I reached around and hugged him. How would he ever recover from this disaster?

Chapter 10

Three weeks later no one was quite so understanding with Dad. He still slumped into the exact same spot on the couch and it seemed as though he never moved. He used the remote control to play his favourite country western hits over and over.

"Dad, I've heard 'Wasted Days and Wasted Nights' six times since I've come home. Can I put something else on?"

Dad stared at the imaginary computer screen in front of him, rubbing the half-inch stubble on his chin—not enough energy to shave yet not enough energy to even grow a beard. He wore the same red plaid shirt and jeans with the knees poking through as yesterday and the day before and maybe even the day before. "What's that, princess?" Even his voice seemed far away.

"Never mind Dad."

Mom didn't even say hello when she came in and saw him in his spot. "Really Ray, did you at least call the job counselling service today?"

"There are no jobs out there. I think I'll wait till the recession is over."

"Ray, don't be ridiculous."

"I don't feel like leaving the house right now." Dad's

voice stayed in a monotone.

Mom's voice rose a pitch. "Well, I don't feel like cooking either. I just subbed for remedial English and I *hate* teaching remedial English. . . ."

It was going to get ugly, I could tell.

"C'mon Beauty, let's go out for a while." We walked out to the yard, and as we started to play Stick I could hear Mom shrieking. She was so loud it was hard to understand exactly what she was screaming. *"You always,"* I made out, and then *"You never . . . and even when you do it's not . . . ."* Something about laundry, something about cleaning, and finally something about cooking. *SLAM!* I expected to see Mom storming out the door.

"Dad?" I called after him. "Where you going?"

"Papa's Pizza! I'm in charge of supper tonight."

"Wait up Dad. We'll come with you."

◆　　◆　　◆

Next morning I could see a slight dent in Dad's spot on the couch, but no Dad. I smelled burnt oatmeal and I heard the radio, "Life is a highway, I wanna ride it, all night long." Tom Cochrane! No more "Wasted Days"! I took that as a good sign.

"Uh, Dad. The pizza box gets wiped with a damp cloth and put in recycling," I told him as he tried to fit the flattened cardboard container into the garbage can.

"Thanks. Eat your cereal. You too, Debra!"

"This revolting gloop!"

I glared at Debra.

"I mean . . . thank you Pater, but really I only drink coffee in the mornings. I appreciate the thought. No don't put milk in it!" Debra rushed out the warning. Too late. Dad emptied the last bit of milk into the last cup of coffee.

Debra turned so that only I could see her. She grabbed the sides of her head, scrunched up her face and opened her mouth in a long agonizing but silent scream. Her mouth shut and her face smoothed when Dad walked over to put the cup in front of her.

"Oh. You don't take milk, eh," he said as he watched it sit in front of her untouched. He snatched it back up and dumped it in the sink. "How about I make you an instant?"

Debra turned to me and did the silent scream routine again, after which she calmly answered Dad. "Don't bother Pater. Early class you know. I'll grab a capuccino at the student lounge." She gave me her Vulcan salute, turned it into a wave for Dad, and rushed out the door.

"So Dad," I sighed. With no milk for my Crunchies, I was forced to eat Dad's burnt gloop.

"So Elizabeth," he returned.

"Where's Mom?" I tried to swallow a spoonful of oatmeal before the aftertaste of char could take hold.

"She's meeting with the Dean this morning. Seems he needs to fill a sudden vacancy for an English teacher."

"Daytime teaching?"

"Yes."

"Remedial English?"

"You got it."

"We're in trouble, Dad."

"Yup."

I quickly ate my oatmeal. If I could stomach that, I figured I could tough out anything that was to come. Anything that is but Dad's chili—which was of course what he served up that night. I brought a jug of water to the table.

"My good news is that I was hired for the daytime teaching position," Mom said unhappily. "The interview this morning was just a formality. Dean Forsythe told me he knew I was up to the challenge."

"Good Mom," I murmured.

"Peachy." "Terrific." Debra and Dad echoed my lack of enthusiasm.

Dad continued the conversation with his turn at bat. "Not only did I concoct this feast, today I also conquered the washer and dryer. . . ."

No twitching, no holey jeans, no beard stubble—Dad seemed alert and connected to the real world. Plus there was something in his voice . . . a strange sureness, maybe even a power.

"I folded all the clothes and put them away in your drawers."

"You went into my room." Debra's eyebrows jumped up to touch her bangs.

"Right into your drawers. I wanted to do the job properly—from beginning to end." Dad gave Mom a hard look. "Isn't that the way you want me to do it?" He turned back to Debra. "Of course I didn't know exactly which drawers were which, so I accidentally went into your junk drawer."

"Junk drawer! Hawh! That is my personal drawer and you know it. You rifled through my things didn't you?"

"No. But I found this interesting looking package wrapped in aluminum foil." Dad held up the little bundle I had noticed while hunting for mascara. "Now we all know Mom doesn't wrap sandwiches in foil. It's not environmentally correct."

"Give me that." Debra snatched at the package but Dad yanked it up out of her reach.

"What is it, Debra?" Mom asked.

"I will not subject myself to these military tactics!" Debra sputtered.

Mom stared Debra down. I could see a tinge of pink edging around Debra's cheek. Mom reached across the table for the package and with deliberate slowness uncrinkled one corner of the foil.

"It's a joint, are you satisfied!" Debra hollered.

"No," Mom said. She continued uncrinkling until a skinny, unexciting, amateur-looking cigarette lay exposed.

"I was only keeping it for a friend."

"An illegal substance, in *My* house?" Dad slammed his fist on the table.

"*YOUR* house. I thought it was *My* room and *My* drawer." Debra stood up.

"It is *Our* home," Mom answered for Dad, standing up to face Debra. "And it is completely unacceptable for you to keep drugs in *Our* home."

"Fine—I'm leaving. I can no longer live under this dictatorship," Debra flung at Mom. She stood there, eyeing Mom with a challenge.

Mom stared right back for the longest moment. At last she sat down. "Fine. Leave then."

Debra whirled around and stomped off to her bedroom.

The kitchen went dead for a few seconds. Then my heart started beating again and Dad spoke.

"Uh, do you think, perhaps, we should uh, try and talk to her?"

"There's nothing more to be said." Mom ate her chili. I poured myself a large glass of water and did the same. It didn't seem as fiery as usual anyway. Afterwards I quietly slipped out with Beauty.

"Don't worry, girl," I said as I sat on a swing at the park.

"Debra won't leave. Where would she go?"

Beauty shifted uncomfortably on her front paws. She moved her head and licked her lips as though she was trying to respond. But we both knew what the answer was.

Chapter 11

Debra was packing when Beauty and I passed her room a half-hour later. *She couldn't go!* Flames of chili suddenly licked at the back of my throat and I wanted to throw up. What was happening to us? To everything! My life was changing and I hated it.

I rushed into her room. "Debra, just tell them you're sorry. They'll let you stay. C'mon, don't be stubborn this time."

"Liz, I'm eighteen. It's time." She kept packing.

"But where will you live? When will I ever see you?"

"Anytime you want. I'm moving in with Rolph."

Rolph.

"I love him and we were going to do this anyway."

Rolph.

"It's just too bad it had to happen this way." Actually Debra looked pleased with herself as she folded her T-shirts into her black duffle bag.

I hate Rolph. "But you can't go! I need . . . I need . . . a Halloween costume." That wasn't what I wanted to say, but I didn't know how to explain that I needed my big sister to live down the hall, not across town.

Maybe Debra understood. She stopped folding and

frowned. Her eyes looked into mine.

"Dad never brought the Santa Claus costume home. And Mrs. Bond's already adjusted the elf costume for Marnie." My voice caught and my eyes watered. In a moment it would look as though I was crying over a costume.

Debra's eyes blinked a few times too and she put a hand to her forehead. "I can do Santa Claus. Don't worry." *I'll miss you too.* She couldn't say it either. "Rolph owns a large red sweater which I absolutely detest. With one of my wide belts, some cotton batting on the edges and let me see, a hat. Halloween is when?"

"Next Wednesday."

"Don't worry. I'll fix you up." Debra zipped her duffle bag closed. "Even if we have to do it at Rolph's place." She stood up.

"Don't go, Debra."

"I have to. Come over here for a second." Debra walked to her closet and opened the door. "Entirely yours. I bequeath it to you."

I stood beside her and looked inside. There hung her purple silk shirt and a pair of black leather pants.

"You like the shirt and the pants, well, they're too small for me. You should wear more black, you know. It would look great with your hair."

"Debra, don't go. Please."

Debra hugged me then. "It won't be so bad, you'll see. You can visit all the time. And you have the beast . . . Beauty I mean." Debra smiled at me.

But I couldn't smile back.

Debra hoisted the duffle bag to her shoulder and raised her free hand. "Live long and prosper." She faced me for a few extra moments.

But I couldn't answer her.

She turned away and left the room.

I sank down on the floor and threw my arms around Beauty. She whimpered softly as she struggled loose to lick me.

Later that night, I overheard a telephone conversation.

Dad was talking in a low voice, which made me listen harder.

"I appreciate the call, Rolph. So she got there all right." A pause. "I never thought she was." Another pause. "I didn't think you did either. All kids go through these experimental things though." "Uh huh, uh huh. It may be for the best. Her mother and I just want Debra safe . . . and happy. We understand one another, don't we, Rolph?"

Apparently they did. Dad hung up. Dad and Rolph teaming up—against whom?

Against Mom? It didn't seem that Mom and Dad understood each other in the same way.

"You know I tried smoking cigarettes when I was Debra's age," Dad told us at supper the next night.

"That's hardly the same, Ray," Mom drawled. If I closed my eyes, I could hear Debra speaking in that exact same way.

"But, don't you see, for me it was. For my parents tobacco was the equivalent of marijuana. So smoking was a big rebellion."

"So that makes it all right, does it?" Mom's tone of voice made it clear that it didn't.

"No, of course not. I guess I didn't handle this problem well. I never thought that you would . . . I mean, that she would . . . ." Dad stumbled over his words.

"Look, I see young people her age all day long. Someone has to draw a line with them sometime. . . ."

I couldn't believe Mom—she and Debra were always so close.

"You know it's not even the joint in her drawer that ticks me off so much. Debra's wanted to move in with Rolph for quite a while now. I asked her to wait at least another year . . . " Mom's voice cracked. "But she's in such an all-fired hurry to get away from us. . . ." She stopped speaking and her bottom lip trembled. After a moment she swallowed and spoke again. This time her words came out clipped and bitter. "What really galls me is that she made it look as if it was the drug issue that forced her to leave."

"Let's not talk about Debra any more." Dad reached out and took her hand for a moment. Then he changed the subject, looking pointedly over at me. "What about everyone's good news for the day."

I couldn't think of anything fast enough.

Mom jumped in, her voice still sounding bitter. "Mine is that we had a power failure this afternoon. I had to cancel two classes. What a relief!" I felt sorry for Mom—she usually loved teaching. *Stupid remedial English.* If it hadn't put her in such a rotten mood, this would have never happened.

"How was job hunting today, Ray?" Mom continued.

"Well, I heard they were in need of a programmer over at City Hall."

"So? Did you send them your résumé?"

"Uh, not yet."

"What are you waiting for?"

"I have some good news," I interrupted—finally something had come to me.

They both looked at me.

"Yes Elizabeth. What is it?" Mom asked.

I had picked the only safe topic I knew, one that no one could find anything to argue about. "Beauty is completely toilet trained," I announced. "Every time I mention the word . . . " I stopped and looked over in the direction of the crate. "I better spell it. H U R R Y U P. Every time I say that, instant bathroom time. She's amazing."

"Beauty's a fast learner. She'll make a great guide dog," Mom answered.

"Sure Mom." I remembered Beauty leaping over furniture at Marnie's house and found that hard to believe. "Oh and Mom, you know how you always say I can have a friend over for supper anytime I want to as long as I tell you about it plenty of time in advance?"

"Yes Elizabeth."

"I'd like to have someone over on Halloween night."

"Who—Alicia? That would be nice. We haven't seen her in a long time."

"No Mom. I want to invite Debra. She's helping me with my costume."

"Oh Elizabeth! Debra can come home anytime she wants to, I keep telling you all—*she's* the one who decided to leave."

"Good. So I'll call and tell her."

Dad winked at me when Mom wasn't looking, but I didn't wink back.

◆　　◆　　◆

Although Mom acted as though Debra coming for supper was no big deal, on Halloween day she worked all afternoon making spinach quiche, which just happened to be Debra's favourite.

Beauty and I hung around the kitchen waiting for time to pass. "Can I help? Want me to roll out the dough? I can shred the cheese for you. I know how to run the food processor." Mom turned around to answer me and nearly tripped over Beauty.

Without shifting her position Beauty looked up at Mom and slapped her tail against the floor a couple of times. "Yes, you can help. Go outside, Elizabeth, and take Beauty with you."

"C'mon girl. We know when we're not wanted." I snapped Beauty's leash on her.

From the front yard I noticed Scott setting up his tombstones. Ordinarily I would have rushed over to help him, but since the dance and with Alicia liking him, I wasn't sure I should. When Beauty tugged me in that direction though, I was happy to follow.

"Hi Elizabeth. What do you think?" Head to one side and frowning, Scott eyed his graveyard.

I read the inscription on one of the headstones.

HERE LIES THE REMAINS OF OUR FRIEND RYAN
WHO DIED WHEN ATTACKED BY A FRENZIED LION

"It's fine. I can't even see the speaker wires. How'd you hide them?"

"I'm not using them here. That's all I'm going to tell you. The rest is a surprise."

I wondered about his surprise as I watched Scott adjust a headstone to lean forward. But there was no point in bugging him about it. Besides, I liked being surprised.

He straightened and faced me. "You hungry?"

"Not really. Why?"

"I can't stand it any more. There's all this candy lying around the house and my mother won't let me touch any." Scott rooted around his pockets and found a lint-covered Lifesaver. He looked as though he was seriously considering it for a minute. Then he shook his head. "Wanna come to the store with me for a chocolate bar?"

"Sure." I didn't even have to think about it. This was normal, like old times. Scott strolled along beside me while Beauty strained at the leash ahead. At one point Scott's hand brushed against mine and I felt my fingers tingle. That was less normal.

When we reached the store, I noticed a sign on the door. "Oh great, dogs aren't allowed in," I said.

"That's okay. Wait here. I'll get you something." He went in without asking me what I wanted.

Beauty shifted from one paw to the other watching the store door for Scott. She whined softly when he finally came back out.

"Here Elizabeth." He handed me a chocolate bar.

I stared at the blue foil wrapper. "Coconut?"

Scott shrugged as he tore the paper off his bar. "It's not my favourite either, but you can win a Mustang Convertible with this kind." He took a huge bite, managing to get most of the bar into his mouth. It always amazed me that he could do that. "Instantly," he mumbled as he scratched at the grey spot.

That was Scott for you. Mouth full of chocolate, ready to win. I pulled back the edge of the wrapper and scraped off the grey stuff with my fingernail. **Try again,** the letters underneath read.

Suddenly Scott threw his hands in the air, yelling, "I won! I won! I won!" He didn't sound like himself but I couldn't tell if he was kidding or not.

Beauty barked sharply.

"Let me see!" I tried to grab the wrapper from Scott's hand but he held it up too high. I saw laughter shining in his eyes. Laughter or something else. Did he win or not? I had to know.

I jumped for the wrapper and Scott wrapped one arm

around my back to steady me. "I can't believe I won." He tightened his hold, hugging me close. "Isn't it great Elizabeth?"

It was weird. I felt his arm warm against my back, his breath on my face. Coconuts and Scott.

"Will you just let me see?" I said as I made another attack. This time I managed to snag the wrapper. Scott grabbed my wrist with his hand.

Suddenly his hand went soft and the laughter left his eyes. Around his mouth, his skin lightened a shade, Scott's way of blushing. For one strange long moment I thought something else was going to happen between us.

He let my hand drop and the moment ended. Everything dropped inside me too and I quickly bent my head over the wrapper.

"Aw, you just won another chocolate bar." I shoved Scott's shoulder as I backed away. "And neither of us even likes this kind. Auugh!"

Scott smiled. "You loved me for a minute there when you thought I won the car."

I felt my face turn red then and shoved his shoulder again. "You're such an idiot, Scott." But I couldn't help smiling too.

We headed back home, and for the first block I floated light and happy. By the second block, though, thoughts started chasing each other in my brain. *Hey, what just happened back there? Wasn't Scott going out with Alicia? Did he like her or me?* By the third block I was almost convinced that Scott had only been fooling around at the store, that I had imagined everything else. As I headed up the walk to my house my feet were heavy as bricks and my head felt dizzy and confused.

Debra arrived with Rolph right then—four o'clock just as

she'd promised on the phone. We ate early so that I could trick-or-treat with Marnie.

"Debra's working part-time at the Dancing Camel," Rolph offered as he wolfed down his third slice of quiche.

Debra still minced at her first piece. Beyond "Please pass the butter," "Thank you," and "You're welcome," she and Mom hadn't said anything to each other.

"Where's that? Is it in her field?" Dad asked with his mouth full.

"It's that new place near the Oakville campus. Well, Debra is a waitress. But the tips are great. And she gets to design the daily special posters!"

Dad dipped his quiche slice in a puddle of ketchup, then bit off half in one mouthful. "You have to start somewhere, I always say."

What great buddies Dad and Rolph were becoming. It made me uneasy.

After supper, Debra did her best job ever as Halloween costumes go. Rolph blew up a balloon for Santa's belly. Debra used theatrical face glue to stick cotton batting eyebrows and a beard to my face. Rolph handed over his sweater and a pair of his jeans. "I don't need either back. But this hat I borrowed from a friend."

Now I was supposed to be grateful. "Thanks," I muttered. With Debra's Doc Marten boots and the baggy pants, I looked great.

Beauty sneezed a couple of times after Debra put red lipstick on her nose. Then she licked and licked and licked until her nose didn't "glow" any more. The antler headgear Beauty tried first to shake and then to paw off. Neither worked, but all the way over to Marnie's house Beauty kept lowering her head and shaking it anyway. She looked like a reindeer that was ready to gore someone.

"Oh you look perfect," Mrs. Bond said when she saw us at the door. "Come inside the living room. The white rug will be the snow for the picture."

"Picture?"

"Here, let's just fix Rudolph's antlers." Mrs. Bond adjusted Beauty's head gear. "Stand straight, Marnie. Smile. Say 'Merry Christmas'. That's nice. And again. One more."

"Aw, hurry up, Mom."

Beauty suddenly moved around, bumping me.

"Hurry up or we'll miss Halloween," Marnie whined.

Beauty whimpered a bit, looked confused, and then squatted.

"Hurry up," Marnie repeated as it dawned on me what Beauty was doing.

"No Beauty. Don't. Slow down!" I begged. As if she would stop for that.

Mrs. Bond watched in horror as her snowy white carpet developed a yellow patch.

Chapter 12

"Oh my gosh, I'm so sorry! It's just that Marnie used Beauty's bathroom command. Can I clean that up for you?"

Mrs. Bond didn't answer. Instead she rushed into the kitchen and returned with a bottle of club soda. She doused Beauty's accident with the soda, and when it bubbled up she gently sponged the bubbles away. The carpet looked damp but white again and finally Mrs. Bond managed a weak smile.

Marnie and I set off before we could do anything else wrong.

It was a perfect Halloween night. A full round moon lit up the neighbourhood and the air was still and warm. None of the kids trick-or-treating had to ruin their costumes by covering them with snowsuit jackets. We passed the usual assortment of clowns, fairies, witches, pirates, and devils but there were a few really neat costumes too. One kid dressed up as a computer with a box painted into a keyboard for his body and another box painted into a screen around his head. Another kid had covered herself in purple balloons and went as a bunch of grapes.

Each house took a little longer than I was used to as

everyone oohed and ahhed over our costumes. People seemed more generous than usual with the treats too, so that was okay.

"Aw come and look, Mary. So cute. Santa, an elf and a dinosaur," Mr. Swanson our neighbour said when he opened his door.

"Rudolph!" Marnie protested.

"What's that, dear? Why does your dinosaur have a branch hanging from his head?"

"She's not a dinosaur. She's Rudolph, the red-nosed reindeer."

"That's nice. Here's a bag of chips for Santa, a chocolate bar for the elf and a candy for the stegosaurus."

"Reindeer!" Marnie shrieked.

"He's just joking," I told her. Although with Mr. Swanson you couldn't be sure. "Say thank you, Marnie."

"Thank you," we both said at the same time.

We were coming back around to Scott's house now. My heart started to beat a little faster and my hands became clammy, especially when I saw a pumpkin man sitting on the porch. Scott. I ran up to sock him right in his straw guts. But it really was only a pumpkin man. *Hmm, Scott must be handing out the candy*, I thought. Marnie rang the doorbell and I felt my face light up when the door opened. I tried not to look too disappointed when it turned out to be Scott's mom and she gave us each a toothbrush.

"Can we go home now and eat candy? I'm tired," Marnie complained.

I knew how she felt. Everything inside of me sagged, but I didn't want my last Halloween to end so soon and I was still hoping to see Scott. "Aw c'mon. It's early."

"I'm tired and I'm hungry."

"So eat one thing," I compromised.

Marnie plunked down in the middle of Scott's lawn and ripped open a bag of chips, the largest item of her stash. Beauty quickly muzzled in to share.

"Don't give her chips!" It was too late. Both Marnie and Beauty enjoyed their snack, chewing with mouths wide open.

"I wanna go over there!" Marnie said the moment the last chip crumb hit her mouth. She leapt to her feet with a burst of energy.

"Where?" I didn't even get the whole word out before Marnie tore across the road. Beauty chased after her, dragging me behind on the leash.

"Don't dart out in the street like that," I said, grabbing her finally. "You could get killed by a car."

"I'm thirsty," Marnie complained, as if that were her excuse. "Look at the nice pumpkins here."

Three huge pumpkins, with grimaces lit up in orange and yellow, sat on the porch laughing at me.

I sighed and followed Marnie and Beauty up the porch stairs.

As we stood at the door a rustling noise to the left of us caught my attention. Between this house and the next one I saw some shadows flickering. I heard giggling, and although I wasn't sure I thought I heard my name whispered. "Who's there?" I called angrily. More rustles and giggles but no answer.

"What is it?" Marnie asked me, her eyes as round as the moon.

"Never mind, just some idiots fooling around. Did you hear me about crossing the street?"

"Uh huh. Can I have a drink of water?" she asked the lady who opened the door.

"You're not supposed to take stuff from people you

don't know," I whispered when the lady returned to her kitchen. She came back with an unopened can of pop for each of us.

Beauty barked once and jumped up on the lady.

"Down girl!" It was like babysitting two badly behaved children. The lady returned with a large bowl of water for Beauty. Slurp, slurp, slurp.

Marnie belched.

"Thank you very much!" I told the woman. We headed back to the sidewalk, sipping as we went.

Walking past the unlit house next door I noticed a soaped message on the picture window. "Trick or Treat." How original! I thought I heard Vicky's voice pretty clearly in the bushes near the other side of the house now.

I also noticed a soaped outline of a face with two egg yolk eyes running down the brick wall. *I could learn to hate that girl*, I thought. In fact, I knew I was pretty much on my way.

"Can I eat something else?" Marnie asked as we trudged on a little farther. She rifled around in her bag before I could answer.

"No." Too late—she was tearing into a chocolate bar. "Why do you even ask?" I complained, suddenly feeling very tired and too old for Halloween. "Here, give me your drink can for recycling." I deposited hers and mine into my bag. "We'll turn around when we get up to Mapleview School. And don't give chocolate to Beauty!"

Just ahead now I noticed a large white-sheeted ghost near the school fence. A warm wind blew up and billowed the sheet out like the sail of a ship.

"What's that?" Marnie asked.

A speaker crackled on before I could answer. "Youuuuuu kids," a voice bellowed out. "Youuuuuu kids."

"It's just a Halloween . . ." I began.

"Alwayyys running in the hall!" the voice shrieked. Now it moaned, "Little girl, little girl," and whimpered, "Come here little girl." The billowing white sheet beckoned.

"Eeeeeee!" Marnie screamed long and hard, piercing my eardrums with her shrill panic. For one heartbeat I froze. In the next heartbeat I grabbed onto the back of Marnie's costume, but she yanked away hard and ran into the street, leaving me with a handful of elf-green material.

"Marnie no!"

There was a terrible squeal of brakes.

Chapter 13

"No Beauty!" It took all my strength to pull the leash away from the street. Beauty flew through the air backwards.

The front of the screeching car still bounced up and down an elf's slipper away from where Marnie had been a second earlier. Grey smoke puffed from the front tires. "Stay there!" I warned Marnie.

"I have to go!" she sobbed. "I have to go."

"Don't you move! Wait for me!" I could see the driver of the car cover her eyes with both hands for a moment. Then the window rolled down.

"Is she all right?"

"She's just scared," I explained.

The woman nodded and waved me across the street. I reined Beauty in closely. *I'll teach these two brats not to dash across the street without looking.* "Do you realize you could have been killed?" I shouted at Marnie.

Her face swelled up with tears and her chest heaved up and down. "I . . . I . . . I," she stuttered with each heave, "have . . . have . . . have to go."

"Wha-at?"

"It's coming for me!" she screamed. "Let me go!"

This time I wrapped both my arms around Marnie.

Suddenly a horn blared.

Turning to face the street, I watched the same car vibrating up and down, a few metres forward, while the sheet ghost flew past its bumper.

"Sorry!" the sheet ghost called out to the driver. It was Scott's voice. *Some surprise!*

Marnie hiccupped as she continued to cry.

"There, there. It's only a boy I know dressing up," I explained to her, patting her back gently as she cried. Beauty tilted her head and whined. "You're scared too?" I asked her.

"Would you take off that stupid sheet before you give someone a heart attack?" I snapped at Scott.

"Is she okay?" Scott asked, uncovering himself.

"I . . . I . . . I . . . have to goooo!" Marnie wailed again, shifting and jumping from leg to leg while I still held on to her.

Something made me finally click to what she was saying. Maybe it was the spreading wet stain down her green leotard. Maybe it was what Scott said next.

"Looks to me like you already went!"

"Oh shut up Scott, will you. You're just so funny. You nearly killed us you're so funny."

"Hey, I'm sorry. It was just a stupid Halloween gag. I didn't think I was that scary even."

"Come on Beauty. Let's go, Marnie."

"Aw don't be mad Elizabeth. I said I was sorry."

"Just shut up Scott. This is the worst Halloween of my life." I don't know why I was so angry at him. Scott was just being Scott, anything for a laugh—and me liking him would probably be the biggest joke of all.

Scott turned away and crossed back over the street, where I saw Alicia waiting for him near the school. Marnie was so tired now that she wanted to be carried. Two bags full of candy, a wet four-year-old hanging from me, and a curious puppy pulling at me every which way. I was having the worst Halloween of my life and it hadn't even ended yet.

It was awful having to explain what happened to Mrs. Bond.

"But you went all the way over to Mapleview Elementary . . . that's so far for Marnie."

"Well, it's just that it was . . . ." my last Halloween, I thought, but she was right, I should have stopped earlier. Right when Marnie first said she was tired. "I'm sorry. I tried to make her stay with me. . . ." That sounded lame too. How could I not control Marnie and Beauty?

Mrs. Bond didn't have anything else to say. She needed to clean Marnie up and get her to bed. But her mouth stayed bent in an unhappy slant as she waved goodbye to me.

Oh well. It was now officially over. "I'll put you in your crate, Beauty, and I'll have a nice hot bath. Maybe I'll have a licorice sucker." Almost home now, I noticed a police car backing out of our driveway.

"What's going on, girl?"

"RAWF!" Beauty started sniffing around on our lawn, her nose tossing something white up in the air as she went. Toilet paper! All over, wrapped around and around our birch tree, woven in and out of our hedge.

"Who could have done this?" We walked up the steps. On the wall grinned another egg yolk face—that same message, TRICK OR TREAT, laughed at me in soapy white lettering from our picture window. Vicky—what did she have against me? She didn't do it alone either, probably with Jessica and Lydia. Usually kids soap the neighbourhood grump's house. How could they do this to me?

Had Alicia helped them? What had she said she was going to do on Halloween? Hang out, soap a few windows. No. She wouldn't hit her best friend's house. That much I knew.

I walked in the door with Beauty and heard Mom grumbling to Dad.

"Not enough that I have to deal with spoiled students who expect me to earn their English credit for them, I have stupid teenagers soaping my windows."

"Well the police told them they'd have to clean it all up. That will teach them a lesson."

"Aw Mom, you didn't call the police on my friends, did you?"

"Your friends? No. Never. I forbid it. I don't want you hanging around with vandalizing hoodlums!"

"No chance of that now anyway," I mumbled under my breath.

"What did you say? Speak up if you want to be heard."

"I didn't want to be heard," I answered.

"Then why talk at all! Just to annoy me, that's why!"

"Look, you're just in a bad mood. So you call the police over a stupid Halloween joke. And the kids you rat on all go to school with me."

"What was I supposed to do? Ask them nicely to clean it up?"

"I'd have rather cleaned it up myself." I gave Mom my hardest glare.

Dad didn't say anything but he didn't have to. If he were on Mom's side, he'd have put in his two cents for sure.

Mom crossed her arms and glared back at me. I ignored her, leading Beauty over to her crate. "Here, brush your teeth," I told Beauty and tossed her a milk bone, shutting the door. I stomped up the stairs and into the bathroom.

"Don't you dare fill the tub all the way!" Mom called when she heard me turn on the bath taps.

"It's not good for the environment," I lip synched the words along with her and then watched as the water level rose higher and higher.

◆   ◆   ◆

The next day at school I looked at all the kids around me and wondered. *Had she helped soap my house? Had he?* It felt as though the whole world might have been in on it.

I didn't want to talk to any of them. I saw Scott and might have apologized for snapping at him about the ghost incident, but when Alicia strode up beside him I backed off. I just couldn't face them together. "What for!" I muttered to myself. "Why should I be sorry anyway?"

I ran home after school. I couldn't wait to see a smiling face, even if it wasn't human, and a wagging tail. Beauty didn't disappoint me, jumping all over me and licking my face as usual. I took her outside and that's when I saw Them.

Vicky, Jessica and Lydia were cleaning up the wall and the picture window. Alicia and Scott were picking off the toilet paper from the tree and lawn.

Alicia and Scott. They'd both been in on it. Steel bands seemed to tighten around my chest, squeezing my heart into my throat. My best friends in the whole world. I stared at them for a few long minutes. Scott started to wave, but I turned away. Never again. I'd rather have no friends than feel this, this . . . betrayed. "C'mon girl. Don't pay any attention to the hoodlums and vandals."

Chapter 14

I avoided Alicia and Scott from then on. If they missed me at all though, they didn't show it. How could they have time to anyway? They spent every breathing moment of the day together. If he was drinking at the water fountain, Alicia was right behind him. If she was at the library doing research for a project, Scott was there holding her books. If he was tossing a football with some guys, Alicia was sitting in the bleachers, watching him with a big smile on her face. Once I was shocked to see Scott in the hall leaning on a wall all by himself. I stopped walking for a moment and actually stared. Then sure enough, Alicia came out of the washroom and they kissed. For a long time. It was too sickening.

By the time the stores started decorating for Christmas I knew they weren't going to break up. I love Christmas even more than Halloween—the decorations, the music, the food— and I couldn't let Scott and Alicia ruin the season for me.

Instead Mom nearly did. The first day of December she launched another family mission at supper.

"My good news today is that I read a wonderful article in *Chatelaine*."

"Oh? What was it about?" Dad asked.

We were eating chili again. One hundred and one quick and easy recipes any unemployed father could cook was what I hoped the article contained.

"It had to do with Christmas. Doing away with all the commercialism. I think that this year, since you're not working, Ray, the *Chatelaine* idea would make perfect sense."

"Aw no, what now?" We'd stopped wrapping with paper last year and used cloth Christmas bags. It was neat and ecological but I'd missed the sparkle and crinkle of the silver and gold paper.

"Now don't take that attitude before I even tell you. This will be a great family project. It will bring back the true spirit of Christmas . . ."

"What's your idea?" Dad sounded edgy now, even though he smiled.

"No buying presents this year," Mom announced proudly. "We make our own!"

The fire in my chili suddenly died. I opened my mouth to protest but no words strong enough came to me and my mouth still hung open.

"Oh come on, Sarah. That's fine for you. Do you expect me to crochet doilies?"

"What kind of stupid sexist remark is that?"

"Well, excuse me. I never pretended to be a handyman, I can't build bookshelves or carve knickknacks. The only thing I'm good at is . . ." He was going to say "his job" or "computers" or something else like that. He'd said it often enough before when he'd failed at unstopping a sink or fixing a washing machine. But now he couldn't finish.

"Why don't you read the article? There are a hundred and one gift ideas. Home-baked cookies, babysitting and back rub certificates . . ."

"Fine," Dad interrupted. "I'll read the article."

But it wasn't fine. How could it be when Dad loved buying tons of last-minute presents every year on Christmas Eve?

I read the article and decided I liked the idea of making everyone else's present. I was taking Shop this term at school, and knew my projects would be a cookie sheet, a wooden spoon and a key ring. That would take care of Mom, Dad and Debra. I wouldn't have to brave the sweltering hot mall with the crowds. Or spend long hours babysitting Marnie to pay for it all. That was, of course, if Mrs. Bond ever hired me again.

But I didn't think I'd be very excited by the presents everyone else would make me.

Mom immediately rushed out and bought seventeen balls of black wool with which to knit Debra's present, even though they still weren't talking to one another. And somewhere, I suspected, Mom had stashed another seventeen balls of purple wool for my gift.

Dad never said yes and he never said no to a homemade Christmas. But he started wearing his worn-out jeans and red plaid shirt again and he sank back into his favourite spot on the couch, staring into space and listening to country music.

In the middle of about the fifth chorus of "Wasted Days and Wasted Nights" one afternoon, the phone rang.

Amazingly enough it was Mrs. Bond asking me back to babysit. "All Marnie ever talks about is your dog. Beauty this and Beauty that . . . you are bringing her?"

"Sure." By now Beauty went everywhere with me. I supplied the doughnuts this time to get back into Mrs. Bond's good books, and I decided to be much stricter with Marnie and Beauty.

I explained it to both of them. I showed Beauty the doughnuts and told her in my army general's voice, "NO!"

Beauty licked her lips and shifted around on her paws till I thought she would go crazy. "These are dog treats." I showed Marnie the milk bones. "They're tasty and clean Beauty's teeth at the same time." I gave Beauty a dog treat and let Marnie choose one doughnut. This time I felt in control.

Until I went to answer the phone. I'd hoped against hope that for some reason it would be Alicia calling, but it was a man who had a special on cleaning ducks. I didn't get that and I kept trying to explain that Mrs. Bond didn't have any ducks. The man kept interrupting, "Ducks . . . Ducks . . . No! Ducks!" He sounded frantic.

"That's right. No ducks, she doesn't have any ducks."

"*Air ducts*," he said, emphasizing the T in ducts.

"Oh." How embarrassing. "You'll have to call back when Mrs. Bond is home."

The phone call had taken two minutes tops but when I returned to the kitchen there was no Beauty and no Marnie.

"Marnie?"

"In here. We're watching 'Family Daze.'"

"Does your mother let you watch that show?" I asked as I walked into the family room. "What are you eating?"

Marnie's jaws worked hard on something. She mumbled as she chewed.

"Where's Beauty? Beauty!" I heard the thump of her tail from under the end table. I looked and saw her wolfing down the last bit of a chocolate dip.

"We traded snacks. Beauty wanted people food and I wanted to try . . ."

"Oh yuck, Marnie. You're eating dog food! Spit it out, come on." I held out my hand.

"Okay. It doesn't taste good anyway. Do I have to brush my teeth? You said it cleaned Beauty's teeth."

"Yes you do!" Now I had a handful of wet milk bone bits. I dumped them in the kitchen garbage. "BEAUTY COME!" I commanded when I returned to the family room.

Beauty knew she was in trouble. She crawled forward, paw over paw, centimetre by centimetre, delaying facing me as long as possible. Her whole body said sorry.

But I wasn't accepting her apology. "BEAUTY!"

She was halfway out from under the end table when she very quickly stood up. And an amazing thing happened. She lifted up the table with the end part of her body.

I pushed her back down to avoid broken furniture and pulled her out the rest of the way. "Beauty. Oh my gosh! You've grown." The last time I'd babysat, Beauty had fit comfortably under the end table. And that was only three months ago! "When did you get so big?" Beauty flipped on to her back and begged me to pat her stomach. I couldn't help it. I had to forgive her.

Time was passing too quickly.

It shouldn't have shocked me when a couple of days later Dad announced he needed to take Beauty to the Canine Vision Centre for her first assessment.

"Today? Now? So soon?" A cold fist grabbed my stomach.

"Didn't I tell you about that last week? I'm sure I did. Anyhow, you read the puppy manual, you knew it was coming."

"But Dad, she'll never pass their tests. She keeps stealing doughnuts no matter what I say to her. She jumps on people and with children, well, she throws Marnie to the ground almost constantly."

"You're not planning for her to fail so that you can keep her are you, Elizabeth?" Dad looked at me.

"Well, no. I never thought . . ." My voice rose and words tumbled out too quickly. "I just meant that Beauty maybe needs more time. Different dogs have different development times . . . didn't you read that in the puppy manual?"

"The trainer will decide that. All the foster pups go back at six months."

I couldn't say anything else. I didn't trust my voice.

"Princess, we still have at least another six months with her."

"Six months! That's not enough. She's *my* dog, no matter what they say. *My* dog." I left the kitchen and ran up the stairs to my room. Familiar paw steps followed.

I flung myself across my bed and Beauty jumped up on top of me. "Stop girl. You can't." Her pancake tongue lapped at my face. "You're tickling me, stop! Get off!" In spite of everything, I laughed as I flipped over and she kept licking me. Beauty always managed to cheer me up.

There was a soft knock at my bedroom door. "Elizabeth, I'm sorry, honey. It's really time."

"Don't worry about that stupid old test, it doesn't mean anything," I whispered to Beauty.

Dad came in and snapped the leash on her. "Six more months, princess, maybe even more. Try not to think about it."

It was hard not to. That day, for the first time in my life, I wanted Christmas never to come. Neither did Mom. She only had about four centimetres of black sweater knit, and after school she came home with a mountain of papers. She sighed heavily as she piled them on the kitchen table.

"How's Debra's sweater coming?" It was the wrong

thing to ask her but I felt rotten about Beauty and needed to spread that rottenness.

"I don't know when I'll find time to finish it. I'd forgotten that with two classes, there are only forty papers to correct. With six there are, well, all of these."

We heard the door slam then and Beauty bounded into the room.

"How's it going, girl? Oh Beauty, I missed you." Beauty missed me back with her nose and tongue, lapping at me and nuzzling me each time I stopped patting her. Ordinarily we'd have been apart almost the same amount of time while I went to school, but this felt horribly different. "Friends, Beauty?" I held out my hand and she threw her huge paw into mine. "Good girl."

"How did she do, Ray?"

"Fine for the most part. She's spooked by raised surfaces though. They tested her walking over a sheet of bumpy Plexiglas. She insisted on walking around it."

"Why would she do that?'

I knew. Rollerblading. "Why does she have to walk on bumpy Plexiglas anyway?" A mixture of guilty relief and anger made me blabber on. "How many blind people like to walk across Plexiglas? Is there ever any Plexiglas on the ground, bumpy or not?"

"Well, she wouldn't cross their wooden plank walk either, it was the strangest thing."

"What does it matter?

"Don't you remember in the puppy manual? Guide dogs need to walk in a straight line. Over sewer grates, heating vents, the works."

Should I tell them? I couldn't. "My dog is not afraid. She's just too smart for them. Who cares if they don't want her as a guide dog. I like Beauty just the way she is."

"When are you going to grow up and stop thinking only of yourself?" Mom said in a small dry voice.

"You're the one who only thinks of herself! C'mon Beauty. Let's get out of here."

Chapter 15

Slamming the door behind us felt good. So did running down the street at top speed. The sun was sinking in the sky, blazing an orange trail among the purple clouds. Beauty bounded up and down, her ears back against the wind, puffs of her breath smoking up around her. We came to the first curb and Beauty bounded around the sewer grate.

I slowed down then. Sure enough at the next grate and the next she still avoided walking across the steel bars. We came to the schoolyard and I picked up a stick to throw for her. It hurtled through the air and Beauty chased after it. Moments later she ran towards me, the stick in her mouth. I held out my hand and she dropped it in. Was it only last month when I needed to wrestle her for it? "Good girl. Good, good dog."

Beauty barked sharply and gazed at me. Her eyes asked me, told me even, to hurry up and throw the stick. I hurled it away. Over and over, Beauty was tireless and each time she did exactly as she was supposed to, dropping the stick into my hand. Elizabeth 10, Beauty 0. Beauty was finally learning to obey. Did that have to make Beauty the loser?

She followed me over to the swings. I sat on one of the

metal rectangles and helped Beauty up onto my lap. She filled my arms she was so big. As we gently swayed back and forth, I held on with one hand and hugged Beauty with my other arm. The purple clouds clustered thickly now as the sun passed completely below the horizon. The fiery trail of sunlight softened into melted butter. I stroked her head slowly. "You're so smart, Beauty. Too smart." Beauty interrupted by licking my face.

I squeezed my eyes closed and let her lap at me for a few moments. Then I took her muzzle in my hands and looked straight into those caramel-coloured eyes. "You'll make a great guide dog. I have to train you. You understand girl, don't you?" Anything less would be selfish, Mom was right. Watching the sky darken, I suddenly knew that so clearly. I leaned my head against hers for a while. And then it was dark and cold. "C'mon Beauty, we better go home."

This time we walked slowly. Before we came to the first sewer grate I coiled the leash around my fist, taking up all the slack. Very close to me now, Beauty was forced to walk where I walked, over the sewer. "It's all right, girl. See? I'm not wearing Rollerblades so I won't fall." I reached into my pocket for the milk bones I always kept there now. "Here you go."

Beauty snapped up the treat immediately. We moved more quickly now and I let her have the full length of the leash. We came to the next curb and I allowed her to lead. She hesitated and walked around the edge of the sewer. "No, Beauty!" I yanked back at the leash. Beauty jumped and pulled at it, still avoiding the grate. I rolled the leash around my fist. "It's all right, girl. Calm down. Look!" I stood over the grate and made Beauty stand beside me. At the third sewer grate, Beauty still balked, but she was improving. "I'll practise with you Beauty. At your next assessment, walking on Plexiglas will be a breeze."

Mom was eating a Queenie's burger when we got home. Her stack of papers was divided into two now and she was scribbling madly on one of them. Dad at the other side of the table motioned me towards my seat. "A queen size burger, fries and a shake, did I get all the right things?" he asked.

The right things? A styrofoam container, a cardboard cup, and a waxy paper one with a plastic straw—did he want to start a fight with Mom? "This is perfect, Dad. What's the occasion?"

"Mom needs to get some marking done. I volunteered to take care of supper."

Mom didn't comment, she just kept scribbling. Sigh! Another paper to the finished pile.

Dad bit into his chicken sandwich and flipped through a sales flyer. I fed Beauty and put her in the crate.

"Will you look at this?" Dad suddenly brightened. "Here's a PC with 486 CPU and 135 megabytes. The CD-ROM is included. How much do you think it goes for? Eh, Sarah? How much do you think it goes for?"

"Too much," Mom answered, not even looking up from her marking.

"Thirteen hundred. No interest, no payments till March. The perfect family Christmas present. Elizabeth could do all her homework. You could record your grades . . ."

"Ray, I thought we agreed that we were making Christmas presents."

"We never agreed. I read the article. That's all I agreed to."

"This is wonderful. I'm the only one trying to make this family work. Every idea I come up with, someone tries to trash."

"Maybe they're not such great ideas."

I agreed with Dad. Maybe Mom did in that moment too. She looked beaten, tired. Her shoulders hunched forward.

"Without anyone's cooperation of course none of my projects are going to work. Now, with what were you planning to buy this expensive electronic toy?"

"My severance. For heavens sake, we're not broke. I have a year's salary in the bank. Come on, Sarah. It's Christmas."

"No, absolutely not. It's not a family present, it's a present for you. Elizabeth, what would you rather have for Christmas—a personal homemade gift or this computer?"

Seventeen balls of purple wool probably never knit into anything or a computer. Gee, this was a toughie. "Well, Mom, I've made all my presents for the rest of the family but to be honest, I'd love the computer."

"You're just saying that because you're mad at me. The answer is still no. Unconditionally. Irrevocably." She flipped over the next paper and starting making some ticks. "And Elizabeth—when you're finished your hamburger, rinse out the container. We can use it to pack our lunches tomorrow."

Mom stayed at the table correcting. And when I got up the next morning she was still there, only now she was knitting. She bit her lip as the needles click-clicked together. In the background I heard Freddie Fender wailing about his wasted days and wasted nights. "I'll never get Debra's sweater finished," Mom complained.

"Debra needs another black sweater?" Dad asked, raising his eyebrows to show that he didn't think so.

"I suppose not. I just thought making her something this year would show her . . ."

"How much we love her?" Dad finished. "Wearing your

fingers out may make you feel you're showing her love. I say we give her something else."

"What?"

"Our support," Dad answered.

"I meant for a Christmas present."

"I did too. What does every young couple that age need?" Dad asked.

"You want to give her money when you're out of work?"

"You want to knit her sweaters when you're teaching so many courses?"

Another big sigh.

"Some of your projects are great. But sometimes what looks good on paper doesn't work in real life. Will you just think about it?"

Mom shrugged her shoulders.

"Sarah, I can't make presents. I need to buy things." Dad sighed this time and left the room.

"Mom?"

"Oh shoot, I missed a purl. Yes Elizabeth."

"I just wanted to tell you I *was* mad at you last night about having to give up Beauty."

"Yes. I'm sorry you've grown so attached to her."

"But Mom. I do want the new computer. If we can afford it, I mean."

"But it's really for Dad, we all know that."

"But I think Dad needs it."

"Needs is a strange word. Nobody needs a computer, it's not like food or shelter."

"I think it would cheer him up."

Mom stopped knitting and jabbed the needles into the ball of wool. She frowned. "Maybe you're right, Elizabeth. Maybe I do only think about myself."

"That's not true, Mom. You think about the whole planet

most of the time. Only right now, I think Dad needs you to think about him."

"Thirteen hundred dollars to cheer him up. Elizabeth, I buy a new book and it cheers me up. That never costs more than thirty dollars."

"Well, I will be able to play some neat games on it."

"Sure and you'll be able to do your homework, I've heard it all before. You know what would cheer me up right now?"

"What?"

"If you could hide Dad's *Country Hits* CD."

"No more wasted days and wasted nights?" I asked.

"No more."

"It's a deal. First chance I get, when he's not looking, I'll hide it in one of Debra's drawers. He'll never look there again."

"Thank you!"

"Oh and Mom . . ."

"Yes?"

"Beauty may have failed her first assessment, but I'll work with her. I can get her to walk on anything."

Mom frowned and then smiled, putting her hand on top of mine. "I never for one moment doubted you could."

Chapter 16

"I can't believe Mom still hasn't talked to Debra, I mean really talked, for almost two months." Beauty sat there watching me brush my hair, listening with her head cocked. "Is that stupid or what? I mean, she misses Debra so much." Beauty snatched up Igor in her mouth, leapt forward and deposited the mangled monster on my lap. I looked at the stuffed creature. Debra had done an excellent sewing job on it. The stitches hardly showed, but still it was worn from Beauty's roughhousing. "I miss Debra."

"RAWF!" Beauty grabbed Igor from my lap and shook it.

"You're not listening!" I complained to her. "Oh what's the use, you're not human. You don't understand." I caught hold of Igor's body with Beauty's mouth still attached to the bottom. We played tug of war and Beauty's silly game made me forget missing Debra and that other heavy loneliness that was eating at me.

Bumping into Alicia at school brought back that heaviness again. I wanted to blurt out to her that my father had lost his job, that Debra had moved in with Rolph, that I didn't think I could bear giving Beauty back when it came time—I wanted to share all these terrible things with her, to have her nod her head and say "Gee that's rough," or to say nothing at all, to just listen.

"Excuse me," Alicia mumbled.

I turned my head away from her just as I had every other time we'd met for the past couple of months.

I'm just as stupid as Mom, I suddenly realized.

"Hi," I finally called out when Alicia was almost halfway down the hall. She didn't have a chance to answer. Or at least that's what I hoped. Maybe she was mad at me too, what with Mom calling the police on her and me snubbing her. *I'll just try again,* I thought. It was a little more difficult next time, though, because Vicky tagged alongside of her.

"Hi. How's it going?" I called. When I finally forced myself to say the words they came out a little too loudly.

Vicky's face opened into a kind of fish mouth expression but I didn't care about her.

Alicia looked puzzled at first, as though she were wondering where the strange voice was coming from. Finally she answered, also a little loudly, "Pretty good. How about you?"

"All right. See you around." Not exciting stuff, and it felt really stiff and unnatural. I hoped this would get easier.

A couple of hours later, both Alicia and Scott strolled towards me, hand in hand. For all the times I'd seen them like this, by now it should have stopped hurting.

I squeezed my eyes shut and took a deep breath. "Hi Scott. Hi Alicia." This time my voice came out in a soft, apologetic squeak.

Scott broke into a grin. Alicia smiled. But I wanted more. I wanted them to explain why they'd soaped and egged my house. I wanted a perfectly logical explanation that showed they were still my friends and that the whole thing had been a misunderstanding. I didn't know how to ask for all that so I said the first thing that came into my mind. "Scott, do you know if goldfish sleep?"

"What?" Scott made a strange face. "Goldfish. Sure they do. Just because they don't have eyelids, doesn't mean they don't sleep. Haven't you ever noticed them sort of hovering in one spot near the bottom of the bowl?"

"Now that you mention it, yeah I have. Thanks Scott."

"No problem. You sure are weird Elizabeth." His eyes were smiling when he said that and I noticed his skin colour lighten around his mouth. The old Scott blush.

I suddenly felt happy seeing it. I knew I wasn't just another joke to him. My skin felt hot too now.

"She sure is weird," Alicia repeated, grinning. She didn't seem to notice anything of what was going on between Scott and me.

"See you, Elizabeth," Scott said softly.

This wasn't exactly what I had planned. "I'll call you, Alicia!" I said at the last minute.

"That'd be great," she called back to me.

Maybe I could just let Halloween go. Yeah, that's what I would do. If it was no big deal to them, I would make it no big deal to me. Anyway, after not talking for so long, just those simple hello's felt great. At supper I wanted to tell Mom and Dad, but they had even more amazing news themselves.

"You'll never guess, Elizabeth. Your father and I went to look at the computer that was on sale at Futures. Just to look, mind you, not to buy—and you know how Dad asks questions, and the salesman . . ."

"Didn't know the first thing about the product he was selling," Dad continued for Mom. "So I asked for the manager. And he didn't seem to know too much more."

"So the manager started talking to your father about

how difficult it was to keep up with all the new technology. One thing led to another till finally the manager offered him a job."

"I won't make nearly as much as I did at Regal Trust. But with the store being in the neighbourhood, I won't have to commute."

"That's great, Dad. I bet you'll get a discount on everything we buy there too."

"Yes. Let's hope your father has some salary left when he leaves the store."

"I've got some good news too," I finally began. "I started talking to Alicia and Scott again."

"You mean you weren't speaking with them? So that's why they haven't been around lately—did you have an argument?"

"Mom, you know why. They egged and soaped the house."

Mom's eyebrows raised into question marks. "Whatever gave you that idea?"

"The day after Halloween, they were here cleaning up around the outside of the house because the police made them."

"Yes, but not because they vandalized our house. They were involved in some prank at Mapleview Elementary. The police officer told me something about them haunting the school grounds as the ghost of the principal that died there. Mr. Huntington wasn't it? The officer thought cleaning up our house was suitable punishment for that too."

"Oh no!" Now I had my perfectly logical explanation. Two months of my life I had let go without my best friends over something so stupid—I felt like a total idiot. I should have asked Alicia and Scott. I should have given them a chance.

"Where are you going Elizabeth? It's dark out."

"I won't be long, Mom. I'm just taking Beauty for a walk over to Scott's house." I couldn't wait a moment longer to clear everything up with both Scott and Alicia. Only Scott first because he lived next door.

Scott first. Was that really only because he lived next door? I snapped Beauty onto her leash, and as we walked across his driveway together I felt a liquid electricity flow through me, lighting up my body. I knocked on Scott's door, afraid that the light would show up on my face. The door opened and I couldn't say anything for a moment.

"Can you come out?" I finally asked Scott. It was something I'd asked a million times in our sandbox days together. Only this time I added, "For a walk?" instead of "to play."

He didn't smile or laugh or make a joke the way he might have. "Sure," he answered softly. He grabbed a jacket and threw on a baseball cap.

I was happy he didn't make a big deal out of me showing up. Even though it was a big deal. We strolled along together, Beauty loping ahead.

"Your dog is great," Scott said to me.

"Yeah, but she's not mine forever."

"I don't know how you can do that. Give her up and all. You're a special person, Elizabeth."

"I'm not special at all." We were coming to the first curb with the sewer grate. "Listen Scott, Beauty's afraid of crossing rough surfaces. Could you help me out with her?"

Beauty turned towards me. Her caramel eyes looked disturbed. "What do I do? Go around or across?" they seemed to be asking me.

"Go girl," I told Beauty. She hesitated till Scott and I caught up to her. Beauty leapt around me and barked. Then she danced around us, with the leash wrapping around Scott's and my legs. It became like one of those stupid gum commercials. Beauty ran around us one more time and suddenly we were tied together. Scott laughed, and when Beauty tried to wind around us a third time, I fell against him.

"Beauty!" I complained.

Scott caught me and smiled. I smiled back at him, and realized that the dark fuzz on his lip didn't bother me any more. I touched it lightly and Scott put his face closer to mine. And then it happened.

He moved even closer and kissed me. It wasn't like what Debra and Rolph did in her room that night. It was such a quick brush of his lips against mine that it felt almost as though a butterfly had fluttered against my mouth for a few seconds and then flown away. I liked it, but still shocked even myself when I moved my mouth closer to his and kissed him back. Quickly enough the butterfly flew away again and I felt my face flush hotly.

"Elizabeth?"

I couldn't look Scott in the eyes, but he put his fingers under my chin and lifted my head till I had no choice. "I wanted to see you because I needed to explain, you know, about Halloween," I told him.

Scott nodded.

"I couldn't understand why you would soap and egg my house."

"What? But I didn't!"

"I know that now. I wanted to make up with you and Alicia because I missed you. And then my mother explained about you cleaning up the next day."

Beauty interrupted us, leaping onto my legs, making the leash around Scott and me tighten.

"Well, it was pretty stupid scaring that little kid like that. I thought that's what you might have been steamed about."

I shook my head. "Scott, I want to be friends again with Alicia too . . . only now . . . . Stop it Beauty! Will you go around the other way." I forced her to unwind the leash from around Scott and me. It was much easier to talk to Scott when we weren't tied together.

"I like Alicia too." Scott shook his head and frowned. "But I can't help it. You're here now and I like you . . . more."

"But you're Alicia's boyfriend right now."

Scott grabbed my hand. "I guess I can't be any more."

He didn't let go of my hand until we reached the next sewer grate. For this one I let Scott take Beauty's leash and I stood on the grate with a milk bone.

"Come on girl." The lure of food helped Beauty make her decision. She walked gingerly across the grate as I pulled the dog treat a little farther ahead.

Scott took us across some streets that had bumpy manhole covers. With the two of us working together we were able to coax and bribe Beauty across.

Finally it became too dark and Scott walked me home. At the foot of the stairs we stopped, Beauty jumping around to get our attention. Scott bent his head and I knew what was coming. I closed my eyes and this time Scott kissed me longer. Beauty pushed against me to finally end it.

"What are we going to say to Alicia?" I asked him.

"I don't know Elizabeth. I don't know anything."

Chapter 17

"Rolph Meyer speaking. Hello, hello. Hello?"

I didn't expect to get *him* answering the phone. It took me a second to recover. "Hello Rolph? Is Debra there?"

"Little sister! How are you? Just a moment, I'll get her."

"Just fine," I muttered into the receiver. I hate it when someone asks you a question and doesn't wait for the answer. *Rolph.* In the background I heard Debra say "You're kidding!" to whatever Rolph had told her.

Then I heard her voice in the receiver, all breathy from running. "Liz? Hi!" She sounded happy, excited even, to hear from me. "Is everything okay?"

"Yeah, sure. I just needed to ask you some stuff. It's about guys."

"Oooh, sounds serious. Why don't you come for supper? Rolph can make his fettuccine."

"No. I need to know fast. Scott kissed me."

"Good going, Liz!"

"But he's still going with Alicia."

"Mmm. The plot thickens."

"I don't want Alicia mad at me."

"C'mon, you and Scottie have always had a thing for each other."

"She's going with him, Debra. What do I do now? Should I tell her?"

"Depends. Are you planning to do it again?"

"Do what?"

"Kiss. You know. Was it a one-time thing or are you declaring eternal love for each other?"

"I don't know. He kissed me three times." I didn't want to tell Debra that one time I started the kiss.

"You have to tell her, Elizabeth, before someone else does."

"What should I say?"

"Be honest. She'll probably be angry for a while."

"Hmm."

"Rolph always says 'Relationships need working at.'"

Rolph. "Um, Debra, if you go with someone, I mean a guy, can you still be friends?"

"Of course. Rolph and I are the very best of friends."

Rolph. I remembered how much he enjoyed blowing her to smithereens in the Virtual Reality game. Then I saw Mom walking through the hall and had an idea. "You know what Rolph says about relationships?"

"Yes."

"Well, Mom wants to talk to you. Can you hold for a second?"

Debra blew a big sigh into the phone. "Sure," she finally answered.

I put my hand over the receiver. "Mom, Debra's on the phone for you."

"Debra?" she called back astonished.

"Yeah. Uh, bye Debra, here's Mom." Well, everything I had said was true. I knew Mom wanted to talk to Debra. Maybe nothing particular at that moment, but I hoped once they got going they'd both find plenty to say. And I headed off for bed before anyone could get me for it.

Be honest with Alicia, that's what Debra had advised and she was way more experienced at this kind of thing than I was. Next morning I put on Debra's black leather pants and purple silk shirt for courage. I didn't know when I would get a chance to speak to Alicia before Scott or anyone else did, so I hid out in the girls' washroom between classes.

"Hey Elizabeth, leather pants! Biker woman—I like it!"

"Uh thanks, Alicia."

"You've been wearing mascara lately too!" Alicia took out her wild cherry lip balm and dipped her finger in the little pot. "Is there a new guy in your life? You look great."

"New guy. Hmm. No." *Be honest,* I repeated Debra's advice to myself. *But Scott isn't new,* I argued back. "Listen Alicia, I'm sorry about you having to clean up my house after Halloween. If my mother hadn't called the police . . ."

"What are you talking about?"

"You know, when you came to our house and had to pick up all the toilet paper."

Alicia frowned for a second. "Oh right. But your mom was cool. She gave us all hot chocolate and cookies when we were through. Even Vicky felt like a dork for soaping your windows." Alicia faced the mirror, spreading the wild cherry over her lips.

I twisted my mouth around trying to figure out a way of saying the stuff I needed to tell her. "Yeah, well," I said softly, "I was mad at you because I thought you'd helped her."

Alicia stared at me, her lip-balmed finger suspended halfway between the pot and her mouth. "Elizabeth—I'm your friend! I'd have talked her out of it if I'd been with her. You know that."

~ 128 ~

"Maybe. Only I thought you liked Vicky better than me. She's more exciting."

"No." Alicia picked up the balm again. "I do like her but she can be a bit of a pain too, sometimes." After a second, Alicia turned to the mirror again, spreading the balm over her lips.

You have to tell before someone else does, Debra's voice repeated inside of me. Just when everything was going so well, now came the tough part. I took a deep breath. "Alicia, I'm sorry I didn't talk to you for so long, I really missed you . . ." I stopped to watch her expression in the mirror. No change.

"Me too. Do you wanna come over after school?" She tucked her lip balm into her backpack and took out her brush.

"Sure. But I need to explain something to you first."

"Yeah?" Alicia brushed and fidgeted with her hair.

"Remember how you asked me if it was okay for you to dance with Scott and everything?"

"Uh huh."

"I told you it was all right but I didn't realize that it did bug me."

"Oh." Alicia turned and faced me again, her mouth still open around her last word.

"Last night I walked over to Scott's house to explain about Halloween night and my mother and all. And we went for a walk, and well, he kissed me."

"Hawh!" The noise Alicia made was a cross between a sharp intake of breath and a scream. She covered her mouth with her hand. For a long moment she looked at me and I watched as her eyes filled. When they were about to overflow, she dashed out of the washroom.

"So what time do you want me at your place?" I asked

~ 129 ~

softly after she left. Maybe I'd done the honest thing wrong. I needed to think this through, to be by myself for a while. I walked back out into the hall.

But Scott pounced on me the moment I surfaced. "Elizabeth, do you know what's wrong with Alicia?" His words came out in a rush and he grabbed my shoulder. "She ran past me crying."

Honesty, do I try it again? Scott's eyes shone bright and hard and around his mouth there was no trace of a smile. Geez, what did I know. I took a breath. "We were just talking and I explained to her that you kissed me."

"You what!"

"Well, you did! I had to tell her, didn't I? I mean . . . you are going to break up with her, aren't you?"

"Yes, but I should have been the one to do it, Elizabeth." Scott bunched up his mouth and marched away from me.

For almost one whole day, I'd had my best and my oldest friends back. Now once again neither of them were talking to me. The rest of the lonely day at school dragged by and I lived for the time when I could go home and be welcomed and loved by my only true friend.

Dad had started his new job that day so Beauty leapt over herself with joy when I arrived home. I opened the door of her crate and she burst out, knocking me over, her tail walloping me as it wagged. It had grown as thick as a tree branch in the four months she'd lived with us. I stared at it in amazement till she woke me up with her flapjack tongue, lapping and lapping at my face. I patted her long and slow to try to calm her down but it was no use. The moment I stopped, she frantically nudged at me with her muzzle and I'd have to pat her again.

"Let's have a snack," I told her and went for the milk bone cupboard. I grabbed a handful and then slid a couple

~ 130 ~

of slices of bread into the toaster. Before the bread popped up, the doorbell rang.

"RAWF!"

"Quiet, Beauty." I opened the door and stood there, not knowing what to say.

"C'mon Elizabeth, ask me in," Scott said.

I stood aside and waved him in the direction of the kitchen. "I thought . . . I thought you were mad at me after this morning," I explained as we sat down at the kitchen table. "Do you want me to fix you a Chocotella sandwich? I'm just making myself one."

"Sure. I love Chocotella."

I slid some more bread into the toaster and spread the thick chocolate across the toast, cutting them both and dividing the pieces between two plates. "Here," I said to Scott. I poured us each a glass of milk. "Beauty, sit." I held up a finger to catch her attention.

Beauty sat immediately. Her eyes focussed on me only and she licked her lips.

I placed a milk bone on my knee. "Wait," I cautioned. Beauty shifted on her paws and licked her lips again. "Now!" I said and within a second Beauty had snapped up the milk bone.

"Amazing," Scott commented.

"Good girl!" I patted Beauty. "Now if she can master manhole covers and resist doughnuts, we'll have the perfect potential guide dog."

"Listen, at the Conservation area they have a boardwalk over the swamp trail. Maybe we can walk Beauty there."

"Great idea." I stopped for a second. "I, uh, I'm really happy you're talking to me. I thought when you took off after Alicia that we were through."

"No Elizabeth." A dab of chocolate decorated the tip of

Scott's nose. He looked at me with a serious expression but I giggled.

"You've got chocolate on your nose."

"Oh, there, is it gone?"

"Just a little, right there." I helped wipe off the last bit with my finger.

He caught my hand. "I ran off after Alicia to explain." His eyes seemed to search around the room for his next words. "I owed her that. I really like Alicia."

I pulled my hand away. "You're sorry about . . . kissing me."

Scott smiled and reached over. "Never," he whispered and then kissed me again.

"I'm really glad." Now I felt my face burn up. Neither of us said anything for a moment.

Scott twisted up his mouth. "Alicia's pretty upset though."

"This is all my fault."

"No." Scott shook his head.

"I have to make her understand. I want her back as a friend."

"It may take a while."

"We need to stay apart at school so I don't hit her over the head with . . . us, uh, together, you know what I mean."

Scott sighed. "You're probably right."

"It'll be okay, I know it will." *Relationships need working at*, Debra had told me. *Or was that Rolph's saying?*

"I'll make it okay again. I know I can."

Scott placed a hand on the back of my neck. It felt comforting, but also heavy, like Beauty's paw. "I sure hope you're right, Elizabeth."

Chapter 18

A week before Christmas I went shopping with Dad. For him this was really early. Even though I'd made presents for the family, I managed to spend every cent of my babysitting money. I bought last year's Governor General's Award-winning novel for Mom on special, and *Fast and Easy, 101 Casseroles with Character* for Dad at the bookstore after we'd split up. I picked up a Star Trek video for Debra and a rawhide bone for Beauty. For Scott I really lucked out. There was a crowd gathered around the centre court of the mall, so I asked a kid from school what the big deal was.

"Wayne Gretzky's autographing today."

"No kidding!" For a few bucks I bought a puck, lined up, and an hour later had a present I knew Scott would love.

Alicia's present took me searching all over the mall, right up until I was supposed to meet Dad by the water fountain. Then I saw it. I had stopped at one of those little artisan's stands where they sold handmade jewellery. There in the display was the perfect pin, a silver cat and a dog nestled side by side with their paws around each other. I thought it was an omen.

Back at school Alicia always turned her head whenever

I walked in her direction. I couldn't blame her—it's what I had done to her for a long time. But I'd been lonely for two months because of it, and now I wanted the hurting to stop. So I wrote a few lines to go with her present and hoped to get it to her soon.

> *I wish I could just go back to liking Scott as a friend.*
> *And I wish you and I could be friends again. I'm sorry.*
> Love Elizabeth

Well, that was the note I finally stuck onto the present. The other three pages were all crossed out—the words on them didn't make the same sense once they were on paper as they did when they were inside my head.

On the last day before Christmas holidays I hoped to have a chance to hand the package to Alicia or slip it on her locker shelf when she wasn't watching. There was a dance that afternoon, and so it was even more important. I got so desperate I finally approached Vicky. "Have you seen Alicia around? I'd really like to give her something."

Vicky cracked a big bubble in her gum before she answered. "Alicia's absent today." Great, the package weighed a hundred pounds now.

Scott and I held hands for the first time at school and we danced every slow dance together. I felt as though I was on a cloud high away from everything and everyone, without a single problem tying me to the ground.

That feeling lasted till I was alone in my room later that night. Then, with hot guilt, I remembered Alicia snuggling into Scott's arms at that first dance. She'd asked my permission first. I had to try to call her. Five times I picked up the receiver, and the sixth time I actually dialled but hung up at the ring.

Alicia seemed to be the only piece missing to a perfect Christmas.

◆　　◆　　◆

Snow fell on Christmas Eve. At first the flakes were gentle, the kind that rested on the tip of your eyelashes. Then they became heavy, drowsy white blobs, the kind that landed on the ground and didn't melt instantly, the kind that was perfect for making snowballs.

I started rolling one to form the bottom of a snowman. Beauty tore all around, snuffling her muzzle into the snow. "Don't eat it, girl!" Beauty yipped at me but then kept racing around anyway. I placed the bottom of Frosty in the middle of the front yard and then rolled his stomach.

"What do you think, Beauty? Big enough?"

"Puny!" Scott called out as he walked up our driveway. He placed a bag on the doorstep. "Step back, Elizabeth. Let me show you how it's done."

Beauty finally slowed down to watch. Over and around, Scott pushed the stomach ball till it was humongous. "Now this is what I call a snow belly." Grunting, he tried to lift it onto the bottom ball. No go. "Come and help Elizabeth!"

I shook my head but stepped forward and reached around Frosty's gut to lift.

"Put some muscle in it!" Scott commanded just as the snowball collapsed.

"Puny eh?" I laughed and quickly grabbed some of the snow to throw in his face.

"Don't Elizabeth! Help me save him." Scott was frantically packing the ball back together on top of the base. I joined in.

"Now make the head a little smaller, Scott."

Scott actually listened but then decided Frosty needed a second head which made things tricky. "Two heads are better than wha-on, two heads are better than one," he sang as we stuck in the noses.

"Now can I have my present?" I asked when the snowman from the twilight zone was complete.

Scott made a face and handed me his bag from the front step. In it was a small heavy package wrapped in gold foil paper with a huge green bow. I held it for a few extra moments and then savoured the unwrapping, knowing there would be no more paper at our house. I tugged the bow off gently and lifted the taped edges carefully so that I could reuse the paper. Would I like this gift as much as I had Igor? I gave myself an extra moment before I untucked the grey boxflap underneath all the wrapping. I peered in.

"Oh Scott. She's perfect."

"This is a puppy you'll always be able to keep."

A black Lab lay tummy up in a little basket—Beauty four months ago when I'd first got her. It was such a beautiful, realistic carving, I wanted to cry.

I gave Scott his puck which Wayne Gretzky had autographed in gold ink.

"Aw Elizabeth. This is so . . . " Scott couldn't finish, but then he kissed me.

"RAWF!" Beauty interrupted us so we bent down to pay her some attention.

"Look girl. This is you when you were little." Beauty sniffed at my carving, but quickly shifted her attention to licking my face.

◆　　　◆　　　◆

Since Dad needed to work till ten o'clock that night we

were going to have a late dinner. Mom's classes were finished for the semester and all her marks had been handed in, so she was home and in a great mood. She'd bought a live Christmas tree in a large pot.

"We can plant it later," she explained. We decorated it with popcorn and baker's clay ornaments we'd made from all the Christmases past.

Debra and Rolph came to spend the night. His dad was in the Armed Forces and had been transferred to Germany a few months before. Rolph was the only one in the family who'd stayed, so this was the first holiday he'd be spending on his own.

"Rolph's lonely and it's Christmas, so be nice to him Elizabeth," Mom told me when the doorbell rang.

Rolph. I didn't like to think of him as a real person. He was the stealer of my sister—maybe even her obliterator, when I thought back to the Virtual Reality game—not someone who could miss his family at Christmas.

The door opened and there they stood, surrounded by bags and packages.

"Merry Christmas!" Rolph wrapped his arms around Mom and me at the same time, kissing us each on the cheek. I didn't turn away quickly enough, but I didn't return the kiss either. I hugged Debra for an extra long moment.

"Here Mrs. Kerr, my special Christmas bread. I made it myself." Rolph handed Mom a loaf of braided bread beautifully wrapped in cellophane and ribbon. "Also a bottle of wine."

"And here's a poinsettia, courtesy of the Dancing Camel. I just got off my shift there." Debra walked in and placed a fiery red plant on the coffee table. "Do you have the wreath, Rolph?"

"It's in one of the bags."

"Elizabeth, help Debra and Rolph in with their things."

I grabbed Debra's duffle bag and then hesitated over a brown overnight bag. *His.* Where would I put it? Not in Debra's room, never.

I left both bags at the foot of the stairs and returned to the dining room where Rolph was arranging four red candles on an evergreen wreath. "It's an advent wreath. I made it for the table centrepiece." Rolph spoke to me as though I had questioned him on the thing.

We sat down in the living room to pass time till Dad arrived. Mom offered around a plate of hors d'oeuvres, along with plastic toothpicks and cloth napkins. I stabbed at a tiny shrimp, speared it and then stabbed again at another one. It fell off. I tried again. No use. Only one shrimp per toothpick, what a waste. I gave up, sipping eggnog and snacking on little fancy-shaped crackers with cream cheese instead.

Rolph never gave up. I watched, fascinated, as again and again he stabbed at a second shrimp and the shrimp either wouldn't stay on or it would fall off before it reached his mouth. Finally, when after about an hour he was down to the last pair of shrimp, he succeeded. Both shrimp securely speared through by his toothpick, he plopped them in his mouth and a triumphant grin cracked across his face.

Congratulations, you've just beat out a toothpick, I thought. No one else seemed to notice or care. It was kind of funny and I might have laughed, if only I knew Debra wouldn't become some kind of extra shrimp on a toothpick for Rolph.

Dad came in then, overloaded with packages that he put under the tree. One large heavy one he set down in the corner of the kitchen. That package was as badly wrapped as the others, with large gaps between the comics section that Dad had stuck on haphazardly.

Mom took the roast beef out of the oven and slid in the Yorkshire pudding. As Dad carved the roast the rich meaty smell floated all around the house, taking me back to all my Christmases past and making me remember that sparkly tinsel and red and green wrapping paper weren't the only things I loved about Christmas. "Here Beauty, Merry Christmas." Dad gave her the large rib bone.

Beauty watched me to see if I would allow it. "It's okay, girl, eat."

Rolph uncorked the wine he'd brought and set it on the dining room table "to breathe." Then he lit the four candles on his advent wreath. Debra brought out the bowls of vegetables, green beans, and brussel sprouts, Mom carried the Yorkshire pudding and Dad presented the roast beef, sliced thickly, and surrounded by tiny roasted potatoes.

We passed around the food.

"The best news today," Dad offered as he dabbed some horseradish on his plate, "is that I sold three VCR's, five CD players, six Discmans, four personal computers . . ."

"And a partridge in a pear tree," Debra finished. She giggled as she sipped from a glass of wine.

"I received a Christmas card from a remedial student telling me I was the best English teacher he'd ever had." Mom smiled. "It makes the whole miserable semester worthwhile. Well, almost," she added.

"I'm just glad we have snow for Christmas. That's my favourite good thing from my day," I said. I didn't feel like sharing the others. "Plus this dinner is excellent."

"I agree totally." Debra put a forkful of roast beef in her mouth. "Mmm, the meat just melts in your mouth."

"Being together with family is the favourite part of my

day. Thank you for including me in your celebration." Rolph smiled.

You're not welcome, I thought. *And you're not part of the family.* I wondered how long he could keep up this nice act.

By the time dinner ended it was close to midnight, but Dad insisted we open one present as we did every year.

He chose for us, bringing the large box out from the kitchen. "Elizabeth, why don't you open it since I chose." With Dad at least I knew it wouldn't be seventeen balls of purple wool. As soon as I peeled the newsprint from the box, I knew what the gift was.

"The computer, you got it!" I flung my arms around Mom and kissed her.

"Hey, hey, I carried it home." Dad beamed, his old self again, only not twitching. I kissed him too. "Now go and get the other pieces to it. They're under the tree."

Everyone joined in opening the rest of the attachments. Mom brought a staple remover from the junk drawer in the kitchen and handed it to Debra so she wouldn't wreck her nails. Dad began connecting the wires as the different parts emerged.

"Here, let me give you a hand with that," Rolph offered. He reached behind the monitor and plugged the keyboard into the slot.

"Look at all the manuals that come with it." I stacked up the books on the table.

"Voilà, the mouse." Debra handed the little wedge to Dad. "And the wire," passing it to Rolph.

Mom stood apart and watched us, shaking her head but smiling. "Just what I like," she kidded, "everyone working together as a family, like in the pioneer days."

The computer seemed complete now. "All systems set?" Dad asked Rolph.

"Ready and able."

"Fire it up, Elizabeth."

I pressed a switch on the console and immediately the computer hummed.

"Yes, there's nothing like an old-fashioned Christmas with everyone sitting around the piano singing Christmas carols," Mom continued.

Dad faced the monitor and keyboarded some things in.

"What's that about carols?" he asked. *Merry Christmas Everyone!* the screen flashed.

"I miss singing carols," Rolph said to Mom. "We used to do that when we were kids."

"Oh really?" Dad positively beamed as he turned to face us. "You all want carols, you get carols. I picked this up at lunch." He shoved a disk into a slot and keyboarded some more things into his new baby.

"Si-u-lent Night!" suddenly Dad and Rolph were singing. The computer accompanied them with a thin electronic sound.

"Ho-u-ly Night . . . " Arm over arm, facing the screen with a soft glow from the words on the computer reflecting off their faces, Rolph and Dad were cute together. Dad crooned off-key and Rolph sang in his rich deep voice, and as much as I hated Rolph, in that moment I hated him a little less.

Mom rolled her eyes and shook her head one more time. Then she threw one arm around Debra and one arm around me, drawing us in closer.

"Sleep in hea-ven-ly pe-eeace. Sle-ee-p in hea-ven-ly peace!" we all sang.

◆   ◆   ◆

"Where did you want me to sleep?" Rolph asked later as everyone took their turn at the bathroom.

Dad clapped his hand on Rolph's shoulder. "Down in the computer room, we have a great fold-out couch."

Dad seemed pretty happy to lead Rolph down the stairs.

Mom smiled and kissed Debra goodnight. In that moment I realized I hadn't been the only one worrying about Rolph sleeping in Debra's room—and yeah, I gave Rolph another couple of points in my good book.

Chapter 19

The next morning as we opened the rest of our presents, I remembered that I hadn't bought anything for Rolph.

"Here's something from Mrs. Bond," Mom said and handed me a large manila envelope.

"Money?" I asked.

"Just look," Mom invited.

"Wow, this is great." I lifted out a framed eight-by-ten photograph of Beauty as Rudolph, me as Santa and Marnie as an elf. "Merry Christmas from the Bonds" was scripted across in large elegant red letters.

"Mrs. Bond liked that picture so much, she made Christmas cards with it," Mom told me.

"Stop ripping apart your present and come see," I called to Beauty. She loped over, rawhide bone still in her mouth. Instead of licking me to death as she usually did, she lifted up her paw and put it on my arm.

I turned my arm over so she could place her paw in my hand. "Friends," I told her softly and shook it. I showed her the picture. "Friends forever."

Beauty dropped her bone then and lapped away at my face.

"In that same vein, for your Dog of Fame Wall or Hall,

from both of us." Rolph handed me a gift in a bag made of red cloth with black Scotties on it.

"The pattern on the bag reminded me of you know who," Debra said softly, elbowing me.

Scott. What was he doing right now? I took a deep breath, loosened the drawstring and reached inside.

"A collaboration of two great artists," Rolph said as he put his arm around Debra.

It was a comic book. And not just any comic book, it was an original about Leaping Liz and her amazing pets Igor and Beauty. I sat down right away and read it. In the comic, I had amazing telepathic powers linking me with animals. Igor had super strength and Beauty was able to wipe out environmental criminals with one swipe of her tongue or tail. It was silly and it was funny. In the end, Igor, Beauty and I parted forever to fight environmental crime in separate parts of the world. Apart from the ending, I loved it. "This is . . . " I searched for some word, "beautiful," I finally settled for.

"I hope so, I started the sketches way back in September. Of course we added a character later." Debra patted Beauty. "You never noticed Igor in my room?"

"When? Beauty keeps him with her all the time."

"Well she stole him from me. That's how I knew you'd been in my room when you borrowed my mascara."

"No. I never noticed." I stared at the cover of the comic book. "Thanks Debra." I chewed my lip awhile and then finally turned towards Rolph. "Thanks," I mumbled.

"You are most welcome." Rolph grinned at me.

He didn't seem like such a bad guy at all any more. While Mom was opening her gift from Debra and Rolph, I slipped Dad's wooden spoon under my shirt and headed to the bathroom to make a tag switch. Maybe I should have brought a spare tag. I snuck into my room and folded a piece of cardboard from my fine paper recycling bin. "For Rolph. To stir the fettuccine." I stuffed the spoon back under my shirt and slunk back down to the living room.

Everyone liked my presents, homemade and store-bought, but when I handed Rolph his he made the most fuss.

"Why Elizabeth, this is a piece of art. How did you make such a beautiful *objet?*"

"In Shop," I mumbled.

"Look Debra, how the handle is so delicately shaped with just the suggestion of perhaps an animal head."

"Let me see." I peered over at it. The rasp had slipped. But looking at it now I did see the vague outline of a duck head.

"Obviously some of my talent has rubbed off on Liz."

Feeling like the inside of a sweaty old sneaker, I felt even lower at Rolph's next words.

"Thank you so much Elizabeth. I'm going to save this spoon to use the first time you come for my famous cuisine. Are you free perhaps tomorrow?"

"I was supposed to do something with Scott."

"Scotty Dog is welcome too. In fact everyone should come. Let's make it our family Boxing Day tradition."

Debra squeezed me and winked.

Later on I finally forced myself to dial Alicia's number and hold on to the receiver as her phone rang.

"Hi." It was Alicia's voice. This was meant to be.

"I'm so sorry about Scott and me and I have a present for you could I come over right now and give it to you and maybe talk?" Even as I rushed the words out I heard Alicia's voice over mine.

"Merry Christmas. The Jacksons—Alicia, Lorne and Linda—can't come to the phone right now. But if you leave a message after the beep, we'll get back to you soon. Thank you and goodbye."

Alicia loved recording the answering machine message. Oh well. I hung up. Maybe this wasn't meant to be after all. *First I'm mad at her, then she's mad at me.* Maybe things would never be the same between us again. I fingered the dog and cat pin package. *Like cats and dogs.* Even when I'd been mad, though, I'd missed her. I would always miss her.

We ate another great dinner Christmas day—turkey with stuffing, gravy, cranberry jelly, mashed potatoes and carrots baked in a brown sugar glaze.

"My good news is that your mother came up with another of her wonderful ideas."

I listened for a note of sarcasm in Dad's voice, but I couldn't detect any.

"Your mother remarked how difficult it was for the ordinary person to buy a computer after she saw how little even the Futures store manager knew about computers."

"Yes?" Debra asked.

"She thought I should design a one-day mini-course for the college on how to buy a computer."

"That is a good idea," Rolph agreed.

He's an okay guy, I finally decided. *The niceness wasn't an act.* And then Rolph gave us his good news.

"Remember how Disneyland wanted to interview me when I graduated?"

"Oh yes," Dad encouraged.

"Well, some Disney people were in town last week so I was able to meet and chat with them."

"That should be helpful in getting you a job," Mom said as she dipped her turkey morsel into some cranberry jelly.

~ 146 ~

"Yes. It did prove most beneficial. They hired me. I'm to start in early June."

"But . . . but," Mom stuttered. She laid her fork down.

"Which leads me to the very best of my news."

"Oh?" This time Dad did not sound encouraging. His "oh" sounded edgy. His face looked terrified.

"Yes. I've asked Debra to marry me and she said yes." With that Rolph wrapped his arm around Debra's neck and pulled her to him for a big wet kiss.

Total dead silence.

Rolph prattled on. "I wanted to give her an engagement ring for Christmas. But you understand that as students with no money, we feel the anouncement of our commitment is enough."

Mom picked up her fork and quickly shoved the piece of turkey in her mouth.

"Congratulations!" Dad boomed, getting up and slapping Rolph's back. He pecked Debra on the cheek. "So I guess when Debra graduates next year, we'll have a big beautiful wedding."

"I've quit school, Dad."

Qu-uck, Qu-uck, the strangest sound came from Mom, a cross between a chicken cluck and a duck quack, only it was low and scratchy. Her head pushed forward and her neck stretched. Her hands grasped her throat and her mouth dropped open. Only nothing came from it now.

"Mom?" She looked a funny blue colour.

Rolph leapt up and rushed to her. He grabbed Mom under the arms and hoisted her to her feet, accidentally knocking her plate to the floor. Pushing Mom towards the kitchen, he turned her around and circled her waist with his arms.

"What's wrong?" I dashed over in time to see Rolph

force his fist under Mom's ribcage. I looked back to Dad for an answer and caught Beauty nosing for Mom's dinner. "Beauty no!" I snapped. Beauty quickly dropped to her stomach. "Rolph?" He pushed his fist into Mom again. And again. The third time, a lump of turkey flew like a rocket from her mouth. It landed near Beauty's crate.

"Get a glass of water, Elizabeth," Rolph commanded.

I brought Mom the glass and she drank it down, her hands shaking. "Are you all right?"

"No, Elizabeth," Mom rasped. "Your sister is killing me."

"Why don't you come back to the table and relax."

Had Rolph just saved Mom's life or had he destroyed it? I couldn't decide. Rolph guided Mom back to her chair with a fresh glass of water. She sat down slowly.

Dad swept up the remnants of her meal into the dustpan and then dumped it.

"Mom?" Debra called softly.

Mom glared Debra's way.

"I want you to understand. I couldn't let Rolph fly off to L.A. without me so I wouldn't have finished the program anyway. Plus, we needed the money."

"You could have asked us," Dad interrupted. He put a clean plate in front of Mom. She still said nothing.

"Mom, suddenly school didn't mean anything. My instructor hated my work anyway."

"Let's not discuss this any more," Rolph offered. "Your mother is recovering here. We can talk about all this tomorrow over fettuccine."

"Yes. Rolph, I want to thank you," Dad rallied. "Your quick thinking and actions saved us from a real disaster."

Chapter 20

Scott and I sat in the middle seat of our family van on the way to Rolph and Debra's. There was something different about him—he had the same bony face and dark chocolate eyes—maybe it was his hair. Nah, it was neatly combed but that was all. I couldn't figure out what the difference was, but I liked it. Wearing a pair of dark blue corduroys, a new denim shirt with a silk Christmas tie—it had a Santa Claus Grinch on it—he let his hand rest lightly on mine. I saw Mom's eyes in the rearview mirror and moved my hand away.

I felt good in Debra's black leather pants complete with my hand-knit purple sweater. When had Mom knit it? It was miles too big for me so I belted it and wore it like a tunic. She'd also bought me new purple desert boots which Beauty sniffed as she sat next to me. "Don't even think about it," I warned her. She shifted on her front paws, licked her lips and grinned guiltily.

After a twenty-minute drive we pulled up to Rolph's apartment building. There was no place to park so Dad circled the block. It was just as well we had a walk before we got there. "Hurry up," I told Beauty, and after a few moments she squatted. "Good girl. We can't have any accidents the first time we visit Rolph's place."

Rolph lived on the fourth floor of an old rust-coloured brick building with no elevator. The halls were covered with gold-veined mirrors, smudgy grey hand prints and large road-map cracks. By the time we reached his door, Dad was huffing. "Out of shape, aren't you, Ray?" Mom commented in a breathy voice herself.

Debra opened the door. Her black hand-knit sweater also came to her knees and underneath she wore black spandex tights. "Please come in."

The first wall we saw as we walked in was covered in Dancing Camel menus. They were amazing: brightly coloured camel hamburgers dancing, or camels with sombreros advertising tacos, camel salads, camel french fries. "Aw Debra, these are great. You are so good."

"You like them, you can have them when we leave."

I didn't want to think about her leaving, and neither did anyone else, so that ended all conversation for the next few minutes.

The apartment was a studio, which meant that besides the bathroom there was only one room. In an alcove sat a huge brass bed with black sheets. Debra threw everyone's coat on it. Mom turned her back on the bed and walked directly to a tall red bookcase at the opposite end of the room to study the titles. Scott and I checked out Rolph's cartoons on another wall. They were amazing too, in a quirky, offbeat way. Scott's shoulders shook and he chuckled as he read them.

Dad headed for the kitchen section of the room where Rolph stood stirring a pot with what looked like my Christmas present to him. "Welcome, welcome. Happy Boxing Day."

Dad placed a bottle of champagne on the counter where

Rolph could see it. "We were saving this for New Year's Eve. But Sarah and I felt this was a more special occasion."

"Thank you. Would you mind finding a corkscrew in that drawer there and opening it?" Dad started rummaging. "Debra, knock on Fred's door and see if he can loan us his wine glasses."

"He's gone for the holidays, Rolph," Debra said.

"Oh I could have brought some, I'm sorry, I didn't think . . . ." Mom blushed.

"It's not a problem, Mom, really, please don't make a big deal." Debra took out tall green tumblers from the cupboard.

"Champagne from a water glass, how decadent." Rolph smiled.

"Can I do anything to help?" Mom asked.

"We're fine, Mom," Debra answered.

"Is it okay if I shut your toilet lid?" I asked. "I don't want Beauty to drink from the bowl."

"Please, my toilet is your toilet," Rolph answered.

"Could I give her a dish of water?"

"We've used every dish we own, but hold on. Here's a pie tin." Debra filled it with water and set it out for Beauty.

"Please sit down everyone. I need to serve dinner now before my sauce thickens."

Near the centre of the room stood a card table covered with a sheet of Christmas fabric. The dishes on it were plain white, but two candles melted over empty wine bottles on opposite ends gave the setting a fancy dress-up look.

"You can sit here." Debra pointed Scott and I to chairs diagonal from each other. Rolph showed Mom and Dad theirs.

At the side of each plate lay a tube-shaped package

~ 151 ~

wrapped in green and red tissue paper and tied with sparkly yarn. I picked one up.

"It's a Christmas cracker. Rolph and I made them for yesterday's feast and forgot to bring them."

We all pulled the wick from the crackers, Scott and I making loud snapping noises with ours. Unwrapping the tissue, I found a chocolate, a dog pin, a paper hat, and a saying. "Girl who values dog above all else must learn new values." Confucius Debra.

"Everyone put your hats on," Rolph instructed. I noticed he didn't have a cracker. Of course, he must have given his to Scott.

"Here, you can have my hat, Rolph, since you don't have one."

"That's all right, Elizabeth. I've made myself one too." Rolph put on a newspaper pirate hat.

Everyone looked so silly it would be difficult to have a serious conversation at this meal. Or so I hoped.

"I noticed quite a few calendars from California colleges on your bookshelf," Mom started in right away.

Here we go. I rolled my eyes for Scott's benefit.

"Yes. Debra and I have been studying them. The American College of Applied Art offers two- and four-year degree programs."

"And the terms run year round so you can accelerate the program," Debra joined in.

"Can we possibly hope that you'll be returning to school then?" Mom asked.

"I'm not promising, Mom. We have to find a place first. I need to apply. It may cost too much. We'll have to see."

"Don't let money stop you, please Debra. Come to us if you need any. That's what we're here for," Dad told her.

"And on that note, I will pour the champagne. One fingerful for the younger ones. We don't want to corrupt." Rolph poured a little in the two green tumblers nearest Scott and me.

"To a great new life," Dad began as he raised his glass.

"And a happy New Year for all of you," Rolph continued.

"With no more disasters," Mom mumbled as she raised her glass. "Financial or otherwise."

"Live long and prosper!" Debra called out. Beauty yipped her agreement.

We all drank. Bubbly and tangy, like an apple juice pop without any sweetness to it, champagne wasn't anywhere near as exciting as it sounded. But it felt grown up to be included. Scott smiled over at me.

Rolph's Fettucine Alfredo tasted okay. It was basically pasta with a cream sauce, only there were mushrooms in it. I debated fishing them out and leaving them.

"Isn't Rolph a great cook?" Debra asked, looking me directly in the eye.

"Yeah, sure," I agreed, opening my mouth to a forkful of mushroom-covered pasta. I hoped I wouldn't gag. As I chewed I hit one. It was spongy and disgusting the way all mushrooms are, but I got it down. Dad's oatmeal and chili had built up my endurance.

"This salad is excellent too," Dad offered.

"I made that." Debra smiled.

No one talked for a while. And then both Rolph and Mom talked at the same time.

"The garlic bread!" Rolph said.

"When are you going to . . . " Mom started. "Sorry, what were you saying?"

"I forgot all about the garlic bread. Let me just get it from the oven." Rolph donned cow oven mitts, and with that newspaper hat still on his head he looked even more ridiculous. He was starting to grow on me. "You were saying, Mrs. Kerr?"

Debra passed around the basket of hot bread. There were noisy mmms and ahhs and other comments so Mom didn't speak for a few moments.

"You never really said when you were planning to actually get married," my mother began again.

"Next Christmas," Debra answered.

Mom gasped.

"You're not going to choke again, are you?" Debra asked dryly.

"No. Could I please have a glass of water anyway?"

"Sure, but you'll have to drink your champagne. They're the only glasses we have."

"Let me get you a mug full of water." Rolph leapt to his feet.

"Christmas! You're so young," Mom said sadly.

"Do I have to wait till I'm old to do anything?"

"Mrs. Kerr?" Rolph said softly as he sat back down.

"Call me Sarah."

"Sarah, we thought everyone would enjoy visiting California at Christmas and that we'd have a nice quiet ceremony. Doggie will be gone by then . . ."

Debra rocked their card table as she kicked Rolph.

"I mean Beauty will be gone by then . . ." The table rocked again. Rolph tilted his head and raised his eyebrows. "Good heavens, Debra, I know Elizabeth is sensitive about it but it's the truth."

Beauty will be gone, Debra will gone. It hurt too much to think about. "Debra wants you to stop talking about Beauty leaving. I can't . . ." my voice cracked and I couldn't go on. I'd interrupted to save Rolph's shins but the table shook once more.

Scott coughed slightly and nudged me under the table. He held his hands over his ears and when I looked at him, he moved them and grinned.

I nearly choked then. He had stuck a slice of mushroom on either earlobe and instead of his teeth, a crust of bread showed between his lips. Complete with the dumb hat, it was just goofy enough to cheer me up. No one else noticed.

Mom drank down her mug of water and then emptied her glass of wine.

"Sarah and I need some time to get used to all these new plans. Why, up until a few months ago Debra was still living at home. Now, well," Dad downed his wine too, "you've quit school, and you're moving to California. It's so far away. . . ." He sounded wistful. "Can we not talk about it for a while?"

Everyone nodded.

"Could I help clear the table?" I got up and started gathering plates. When I collected Rolph's, I noticed a whole pile of mushrooms near the edge of his plate.

"They're the only vegetable I detest," he explained when he saw me looking. "I put them in for Debra."

Was this the same person who had blasted my sister away nine times in Virtual Reality? It was hard to believe.

When we finished dessert, a Black Forest cake Rolph had baked, he suggested we play picture charades.

"How do you play that?" Scott asked.

"Debra and I will be the artists. We all decide on categories and write down some words or phrases that fit. Then Debra or I draw things to make the others guess the phrase."

"Men against women?" Scott asked.

"All right, if you insist. How about an easy category, one everyone will know. Say, uh, Disney films." Rolph acted as though he'd pulled the category from the air, but he'd said it so sharply, I felt he must have planned it all along.

"You're on, Rolph!" Debra said. We women grouped and quickly wrote out some titles on a paper: Cinderella, Pinocchio, Homeward Bound. "How many did you say we need?" Debra asked.

"Shhh, love, we're thinking," Rolph said. From the expressions on Scott's and Dad's faces, they were having trouble.

The women came up with a few more and then sat back and chatted.

"Really, could you be a bit more quiet?" Rolph asked and gave us a look. Whoa, this was a different Rolph.

Finally the men came up with three. For the first one Debra rapidly sketched a black dog and then an Igor.

"Beauty and the Beast!" I shouted.

Rolph's turn. He started drawing a fireplace, and motioned frantically to the bottom of the flames.

"Homeward Bound," my father shouted.

Rolph shook his head and drew an umbrella.

"Mary Poppins," Scott guessed.

"No, no, no!" Rolph shouted.

"You're talking, Rolph!" Debra warned.

"I thought Mary Poppins was a good guess," I commented.

Rolph frantically sketched a devil then.

"Davy Crockett!" Dad guessed.

"Zorro!" Scott yelled.

They were hopeless. Mom, Debra and I were rolling on the floor. "Cinderella," we all cried, when the time was up.

"Didn't you understand?" Rolph asked his men partners. "The bottom of the fire—cinder, half of umbrella—ella."

"I thought you meant hearth which made me think home. What was the devil?" Dad asked. "That completely lost me."

"I was trying to show you sin, I was desperate. Those were great clues I drew. I can't believe neither of you could get it."

The men's team never improved but the women guessed their films almost right away. By the time we left, Rolph wasn't talking much. He barked his goodbyes as he clattered pots and dishes angrily in the sink. I watched him as I headed out the door. He was twitching worse than Dad ever did.

Dad started up the van while Mom stared out the windshield and shook her head. "Did you see how he acted during that game?"

"Rolph's just a poor loser," Dad told Mom. "But that also means he tries harder to win. He'll be successful."

I remembered Rolph stabbing at the shrimp on Christmas Eve until he finally speared two on one toothpick. Dad was right about trying hard.

"They have so little," Mom murmured.

"They have each other and their Art. Come on, we didn't have much more when we were married."

"If only I knew she was doing the right thing," Mom murmured on.

"Even if she isn't, it's really not up to us, is it Sarah?"

♦   ♦   ♦

When we got home, I walked Scott back to his house with Beauty as my escort. "It wasn't a really exciting night, was it?" I told him.

"Oh, I don't know. I don't like Fettucine Alfredo but the

cake was pretty good. Well, except for the cherry stuff in it."

"Food, food, food!" I punched his shoulder. "Is that all you ever think about?"

"No." He caught my fist and pulled me closer to him. "Picture charades was kinda neat, except we got stuck with the worst player."

"Food and winning." I struggled to free my wrist to slam him again.

Scott grinned. "Just kidding—this is the exciting part." He bent his head closer to mine. That's when it hit me what was different about Scott. I ran my fingers over his upper lip.

"I shaved. First time. What do you think?" Scott asked.

"I like it," I said as I kissed him. "Thanks for coming."

"Thank you."

I left him and still felt like walking. No stars shone; the sky was a black empty hollow. A heaviness hung on to me and I couldn't shake it. *Debra's really going to leave,* I thought as I walked. Then I stopped. "And so are you, Beauty." I reached down to pat her and suddenly my eyes blurred with tears. I hugged Beauty for a moment and touched something hard in my coat pocket. Stuffed in there, Alicia's present weighed me down even more.

"Come on Beauty. Let's deliver a package." We walked on. *It won't be long till I'll have to walk alone,* I thought. Watching Beauty's happy bobbing head, it was hard to imagine.

The Jacksons' station wagon stood in the driveway and every light in the house seemed to be on. I stared at the house for a while, stared at Alicia's window, even thought I saw her shadow cross the wall. I felt so alone. "I can't do it, girl. I can't ring the bell." I ran up the walk, opened the mail box, shoved in the package and let the lid clang shut.

Beauty and I ran all the way home.

Chapter 21

For a long time I expected a phone call from Alicia, then after a couple of weeks I looked for some other sign that she'd received my present. I never saw the pin on her, but I couldn't really look without staring. My best friend—I finally faced the fact that she was lost to me.

The last day of the month was locker cleanup at our school. Mine always needed more cleaning than everyone else's, and as I was sorting out the smelly gym sneakers and socks collecting at the bottom, I found a cream-coloured envelope with my name on it. How'd that get there? Smudged with a footprint, the envelope looked as though it had been around awhile. I tore it open.

> Dear Elizabeth,
> Thanks for the cute pin. I really liked it. I'm not mad at you any more, it's just that Scott still means a lot to me and I need some time to deal with breaking up. Okay?
>
> Alicia

With no date at the top, I couldn't tell how long the letter had lain there. Had she slipped it in my locker door the first day back at school? But that was almost four weeks ago. Quickly I scribbled a note back.

> Dear Alicia,
> You have till Friday, February 14th, 5:00 p.m. My birthday, remember? Bring a pillow and a sleeping bag.
>
> Elizabeth
> P.S. I didn't find your note till locker cleanup day.

Not taking any chances, I stuck my message on her locker with six strips of tape. And then I tried to forget about it, not daring to hope too much.

"Guess what I have planned for tomorrow night?" Scott asked me on the phone the day before my birthday.

"Tomorrow night? Tomorrow's my birthday."

"I know. And Valentine's Day. That's why this is so great."

"I give up."

"Monster Trucks."

"Monster Trucks?" I repeated.

"Yeah, they're at the Skydome and my dad was able to nab two tickets for me."

I couldn't say anything for a couple of minutes.

"Elizabeth, are you there?"

"Uh huh. Scott, I can't go."

"What! Fred the Firebreathing Metalhead's gonna be there, Elizabeth."

"I planned a sleepover."

"Cancel it. We're talking Big Foot, Ramcharger, even the Ultimate Destroyer, they're coming from all over the States."

"I can't, Scott."

"But it's Valentine's Day."

"Oh right! The Ultimate Destroyer sounds very romantic."

"Well, a sleepover could be if I was invited."

"Very funny Scott."

"What are we going to do?" he sighed.

"What time are the Monster Trucks?"

"Nine o'clock."

I thought for a minute. "How about you ask Tyler to go with you?"

"Great idea!" Scott sounded incredibly relieved.

"Scott!"

"Well, we can do something together before. We can go . . . uh . . ."

"Skating, how about we go skating?"

"Skating's good. That won't cost anything. Those tickets broke me," Scott quickly explained.

"And that way Beauty can come. She's going for another assessment tomorrow. Scott, I'm not going to have her another birthday."

"Sure. Beauty's cool."

"But I need to be home by five. My mom will be making a special birthday supper."

I should have told Scott who was coming to the sleepover. *Be honest,* I remembered Debra's advice. *You can't stay for my birthday dinner because I'm having Alicia.* Even inside my head the truth sounded like something that would hurt Scott more. Between Scott and Alicia I kept feeling forced to choose one over the other. Just this once, on my birthday, I didn't want to.

"Happy birthday princess," Dad called up the stairs to wake me up the next morning.

"Would you like to take the day off school?" Mom asked me when I came to the table for breakfast.

"Mom?" I thought for a moment I was still in my bed dreaming.

"It is your birthday today. And I thought you might like to be part of Beauty's assessment."

"NO!" I hadn't meant to use my army general's voice.

"It might make it easier for you to accept."

"No," I repeated more softly. "I just can't, Mom. And besides, it's Valentine's Day. I want to see Scott."

"First Debra, now you." Mom sighed.

I lowered my voice even more. "I'm not like Debra."

"Fine. What time did you say Alicia was coming?"

"Mom, she's supposed to be here at five but I'm not sure if she's coming."

"What?"

"I'll explain to you tonight if she doesn't make it."

"All right Elizabeth. Whatever you say."

On the intercom that morning, the principal wished me and ten other kids a happy birthday. My homeroom teacher made the class sing to me. Thirteen. It felt strange to actually be a teenager. Good and bad strange.

Scott gave me his present at lunch. First he bought me a bag of sour cream and onion chips. "Here, your favourite."

I shared them with him. Then he gave me a small box wrapped in red foil. I liked just looking at the package.

"Go on, unwrap it, will ya?" Scott said. "I can't stand waiting."

It was a small silver heart-shaped locket. I opened it and scrunched inside was a piece of a picture of Scott—his eyes and his nose basically.

"I couldn't find a picture small enough so I cut one up."

"I love it." I reached over and kissed him. It was something I never did in school, never mind in front of everyone in the cafeteria.

"Ooooooooooh," some kids from the next table called out.

When I pulled away, I noticed Alicia heading towards us.

Scott took my hand and pulled me back to him. "Happy Valentine's Day." He kissed me back. "Happy birthday." He kissed me again.

More oooohs.

"Stop Scott, Alicia's coming." I pulled away from him and stood up. Alicia was one table away now. My eyes met hers and she stopped, fidgeting with something near her collar. The cat and dog pin—she was wearing it. Then she turned and walked away.

"Alicia," I called out softly but it was too late. I slumped back down.

"Now where were we?" Scott leaned forward.

"Scott!" I pushed him away. "Be serious for a minute. Alicia saw us kissing."

"Elizabeth, it's time to stop hiding from her."

"Alicia told me she needed time to get used to breaking up with you."

"We've been going together almost two months! How much more time does she need?"

I folded my arms across my chest.

Scott sighed. "Do you want me to go after her?"

I shook my head.

"Okay, then. Let's not fight on Valentine's Day." He kissed me quickly. "Here let me help you put the locket on." Scott took the box from my hand and lifted out the necklace. After he'd fastened it around my neck, he smiled. "Are you sure you don't want to do Monster Trucks tonight? I can cancel Tyler."

"No. Do you know it's my first and last birthday with Beauty?"

"She doesn't know or care, Elizabeth."

"You're right, she doesn't understand. But it just makes everything harder."

After school we went home first and when I opened the door to Beauty's crate I found a note.

> *Congratulations. Beauty walks on Plexiglas and planks now.*
>
> *Love Mom*

"What's that mean, Elizabeth?"

"It means I'm losing another best friend." I dropped to my knees and let Beauty cover me with her wet dog kisses. I hugged her for a long time. "Good girl," I murmured into her fur. "Good girl."

"Hey, is this for me?" Scott asked, ignoring us as he reached for a recycled candy box covered with hearts.

"No, it's for my father!"

Scott dropped the box quickly.

"It's for you, silly," I managed and broke away from Beauty.

Scott winked at me and then lifted the lid. "Aw, this is great. You make it yourself?" he continued as he picked a piece of chocolate fudge.

I nodded.

"Mmmm. Here, have some," Scott offered with his mouth full. "Not you, Beauty." She'd thrown her paws on his lap. Her tilted head almost reached his chest and she pleaded with her eyes.

"You can walk on bumpy things now, but you can't resist people foods, can you girl?" In some ways she was still the same old puppy.

And that afternoon Scott was the same old Scott I'd

grown up with. He made me forget that he was now my boyfriend as he grabbed my hat and made me chase him for it. Weaving and dodging, he showered me with ice when he finally stopped sharply on the edges of his skates. And after I took his mitt, he chased me all over the rink for it.

"RAWF!" Beauty warned him, otherwise we probably would have forgotten her. Faster and faster, around and around. Scott and I were both huffing and puffing when he cornered me against the wooden fence.

"Gotcha," Scott said, looking pretty pleased with himself.

"Oh yeah?" I tried to dodge around him but he closed in on me. "You win, you win." I handed him his mitt.

"I like winning," Scott said just before he leaned over and kissed me.

We played Stick with Beauty for a while too until it started to get dark. When I glanced at my watch, I realized we needed to hurry home in case Alicia showed up.

"Did you want to come in?"

"Well yeah! I left my fudge in the kitchen."

What time was it? My watch flashed 5:10. "I can run in and get it for you."

"Why can't I come in?"

"Because, uh, I don't know. Come in then." I opened the door and looked around. I didn't see Mom or Alicia.

"So I guess this means I'm not invited to your birthday dinner."

"No. Well, I mean, I don't know if Mom made enough. She wasn't expecting . . ."

"Hi, Elizabeth." My mother breezed into the kitchen. "Oh hi Scott, do you want to stay for supper? Nothing special, we're just ordering pizza."

Way to go Mom. I bit my lip and shook my head. "Scott, I'm expecting Alicia," I finally confessed to him, shrugging my shoulders. "She's the friend I invited for the sleepover."

"Oh." It was a toneless "oh," not angry, not hurt.

"I want to work at being friends with Alicia," I whispered to him.

"So do I," he whispered back. "What time are you expecting her?" Scott asked.

"Five." We both looked at the kitchen clock. It was five-thirty now. "I guess she's not coming."

"I'll just order more in case," Mom suggested brightly.

She called Papa's Pizza and then plunked herself down. "What's new with you these days, Scott?"

Newcastle, New Brunswick, Newfoundland . . . and what about those Leafs, I answered in my head. It was amazing how Mom could come up with so much small talk with Scott. I stared at the clock. At 5:50, the doorbell rang.

"Maybe that's her." I looked at Scott, then dashed to the door.

"That will be twenty-two fifty!" the delivery man said when I opened the door.

While Mom paid, I took the pizza and set it down in the middle of the table. Mom returned and took out the cutlery while I got the plates.

The doorbell rang a second time.

"I'll get it." I rushed to the door and opened it for Dad this time. "Sorry, I forgot my key. Happy birthday princess, here." He handed me a Futures bag. "I can only stay for my supper break. Has the pizza come yet?"

"Thanks, Dad. Yeah, pizza's here." I looked in the bag right away. Before I could really check out the present, the doorbell rang a third time.

"Hi, sorry I'm late."

It was Alicia after all, sleeping bag, pillow and package tucked under her arms. I felt like hugging her. Instead I whispered, "I thought you weren't coming."

"I didn't think I was either. Until lunchtime. That's when I knew I was ready."

Then I did hug her.

After we broke apart again we walked towards the kitchen.

"Um, uh, Scott's here," I warned her softly.

"It's okay," she mouthed the words to me, then loudly called out, "Hi Scott. Notice anything different about me?" Alicia grinned.

"New hairstyle," Scott suggested.

Alicia shook her head and continued grinning, this time turning to face me. "Tell me you don't notice what's new!"

"Grape lip balm! No? Oh my gosh you got braces!"

"Yes! Finally! That's why I'm late. The cement didn't set properly the first time. Like the elastics? I chose the colour in honour of your birthday."

"Purple! I like it."

"What's in the bag?"

"I don't know. Dad just gave it to me." I reached in and took out a box.

"It's a program for the computer," Dad explained. "You type in your location and the time and it calls up the star constellations that are in your sky."

"Awesome—we can do it after supper."

"Well, it's a clear night. Let me just go downstairs and load it for you." Dad grabbed a slice of pizza and headed to the computer room with the box.

Mom, Scott, Alicia, and me, how cozy. I felt stupid.

"So Alicia, tell us all about the braces." Mom chaired this conversation too. After a couple of slices of pizza, Dad returned and wanted us all to check out the screen. We marched downstairs.

"Everyone choose a constellation and we'll try to find it in the sky."

Dad keyboarded in our location. We all peered at the screen and then at the manual that came with the program.

"Ready?" Dad asked. "We'll bring the book to make it easier."

Up the stairs we trooped, Beauty at the end.

"We just need to figure out where south is. Anybody see, uh, Orion the hunter?"

"I see it. Over there," Scott pointed.

"All right, so I'll hold up the map this way."

"Wow. There's the one I was looking for."

"Where, where? Let's see," Alicia asked.

I pointed to the sky and Alicia squinted.

"Let me guess. Something to do with dogs, right?"

"Yup, the Great Dog. That's his head, there's his body. "

"Look Beauty, over there. It doesn't look much like you." Alicia tried to hold Beauty's head in the right direction. It didn't work.

"Betcha I know which constellation you chose," I told Alicia.

"Lynx the Cat, of course." She smiled.

"I knew it!"

"Too bad we need to keep running up and down the stairs to look at the sky," Mom commented.

"We wouldn't if we had a notebook computer," Dad offered eagerly.

"Not a chance, Ray."

"Underneath the big dipper over there are the two hunting dogs," Scott announced.

Beauty looked confused, but kept searching the sky along with us till we went back inside.

Dad didn't get a chance to eat any cake, since he was already late. "Save me some, eh kids?" he said as headed back to Futures.

"No way," Scott kidded. And then after the cake and ice cream, Scott took his fudge and I walked him to the door. He pecked my cheek quickly. "Bye Elizabeth," he said softly and then called out loudly, "Bye Alicia, see you . . . ." It sounded as if he was going to say tomorrow, but then changed his mind.

"Forgot tomorrow's Saturday eh?" I commented.

"Yeah, forgot, heh, heh." The skin around his mouth changed colours, which made me think he was keeping something from me. Before I could ask him about it, Scott walked away.

"Scott sure acted funny, don't you think Alicia?"

"Nah," she said quickly. "C'mon, let's go to your room and you can open my present."

They weren't going to see each other tomorrow, were they? I wanted them to be friends again, but not like that.

Beauty yipped at me so I pushed that thought out of my mind and ran up the stairs to my room with Alicia and Beauty following me.

I opened the card first and there was the ticket for Virtual Reality tucked in. I felt giddy I was so happy.

"That's not really a present, I was just saving my birthday present to use with you."

"Oh great! Let's go tomorrow, first thing!"

"Tomorrow?" Alicia seemed nervous about that, which made me feel uneasy again. "Well okay, if we go early."

What's the big deal about tomorrow? I pushed away the uncertainty as I opened her present. "Aw man, this is exactly the T-shirt I wanted to buy you for your birthday!"

"Best friends like the same things," Alicia boasted.

That made me feel good. I threw the T-shirt on over my top and we turned out the lights to watch it glow in the dark.

"Not dark enough," Alicia said. "Let's go in the closet."

We squeezed in, and with Beauty pushing in along with us it was a tight fit.

"What's that smell!" Alicia complained. A coat draped over her head and shoulders, making her just a shape in the dark.

"What smell?" I asked. It was warm and stuffy in the closet, and sitting on a pile of dirty socks, with Beauty panting doggie breath in my face, I thought I might pass out.

"Never mind," Alicia answered. "Look, it's working."

Sure enough the letters lit up. I'M TOO SEXY FOR THIS SHIRT, I read the letters upside down. I shifted a bit and accidentally leaned on Beauty's tail. She yelped.

"Sorry." I moved again and elbowed Alicia.

"Ouch!"

"Sorry." I sat still in the blackness for a moment, the dark giving me courage. "So are we all squared away about Scott and everything?" I finally asked.

"Yeah. It's just like the shirt, and sour cream and onion potato chips . . ."

"And purple nail polish," I continued.

"You have the same good taste as I do, that's all."

I couldn't see her face to know if that meant she still liked Scott in a big way. Beauty whined. "Except dogs are better than cats, right girl?"

"Only this dog," Alicia agreed. I heard Beauty's tail thumping in response. "You don't like the mall as much as

I do, though," Alicia commented after a moment.

"I did have fun Christmas shopping there this year."

"And you don't like Vicky, or Lydia or Jessica." Alicia's voice dropped.

"It just felt like they were hogging you. I never really didn't like them."

"You always made me think that I had to choose, you or them."

I shifted around in the smelly darkness. "I'm sorry." It's the way I'd felt about Scott and Alicia, that I'd been forced to choose and it wasn't fair. "I'll try to be, you know, friendly with them if they give me another chance."

"Well, it doesn't matter so much about Vicky right now."

"Why not?"

"Todd and I, uh . . . " Alicia sounded as though she was blushing.

"You like Todd! Honest!" She wasn't meeting Scott tomorrow. I didn't know how I could have thought that. "But Vicky has a crush on him."

"Uh huh."

"And she won't talk to you now?" I asked, opening the closet door.

"Pretty stupid eh?" Alicia grinned. Her teeth sparkled with their new jewellery.

I smiled too but shook my head. It wasn't too early to start making an effort. "Not so stupid, really."

Chapter 22

"Have you ever done this before?" Alicia asked me the next day at the Cyberforce Arcade. The attendant nodded when we presented our tickets and then led us over to the Virtual Reality game.

"No. But I've watched my sister and her boyfriend play. It's totally bizarre."

Alicia squinted at the strange black pod behind the divider fence. "I'll say. Totally."

"Read the instructions, please," the attendant told us.

I'd read them before so I skimmed through and finished ahead of Alicia. The attendant rigged me up first with the belt and helmet.

"So you know how the joystick works?"

I nodded and the weight of the helmet made my chin want to stay resting against my chest.

"Just practise walking then while I fix up your friend."

What I saw through my visor didn't seem to be much different than what I'd watched on the monitors hanging from the ceiling when Debra and Rolph had played. Except that I controlled which area appeared on the screen by my trigger and by which direction I faced. The view seemed flat—wearing 3-D glasses at a Cinesphere movie gave a more realistic effect as far as I was concerned. And yet it became like a strange dream. I felt disconnected, as though I was floating away from my regular-sized self and condensing into this tiny jumpsuited cartoon figure.

When I spun my head around the different coloured tiles swirled together, making me feel dizzy. "Whoa!" I found my balance again and pushed hard at the button underneath my thumb, shooting my little screen person to the other side of the platform. "Too fast," I told myself. I pressed more gently and led my figure to some stairs. When I continued to press he scooted up, and when I turned around, more slowly this time, and pressed again he scooted back down.

"Are you ready?" The attendant tapped on my helmet.

"Yup."

"Would you test out the communications link, please."

"Hello, hello Alicia. Can you hear me?"

"Loud and clear," Alicia answered directly into my ears. It sounded as though she was inside my head.

"Yess! Prepare to meet your maker, Alicia!" I growled, and heard nervous giggling in return.

The attendant patted me on the shoulder. "Have fun."

"I plan to," I hissed into the microphone, and started walking myself around with the joystick.

"Where are you?" Alicia's voice asked a few moments later. She sounded edgy and lost.

"Not telling!" I did my best impression of maniacal laughter as I snuck up on Alicia's tiny yellow-haired figure. I raised the joystick, took aim . . .

"Aw c'mon. I don't get this game. Where are you?"

And fired! A puff of white smoke showed on the screen in my visor. "Gotcha!" I yelled. Alicia exploded into tiny bits.

"What, I'm dead already?" she asked.

"Don't worry, you'll come back to life." Meanwhile I quickly scanned the red and white tiles to get a jump on her when she rematerialized. I couldn't find Alicia but I did notice the pterodactyl flapping in my direction. Now it was over my head, its huge clawlike feet coming towards me. I tried to duck. "I'm so stupid, I can't believe it," I said out loud and then straightened and fired at the underbelly of the bird. "I killed the bird, I killed the bird, I killed the bird!" In the nick of time I noticed Alicia's screen figure move up from behind me. A flame burst from her gun but I pressed my joystick button hard and zoomed away. She fired again and again.

"Rats, rats! I don't think my gun works," Alicia's voice hissed into my ears.

"Sure it does. Your aim's just off." I raised my joystick and fired three times. The third shot obliterated Alicia again. "Gotcha, gotcha, gotcha. Oh yess!" I made myself move around on the screen, scouting.

"That bird's coming for me. What do I do?" Alicia called. I couldn't see her or the pterodactyl.

"Shoot, shoot, shoot!" Then I saw her. The dinosaur bird flapped away with the Alicia figure tucked in its claws.

"Awwww! When does this thing drop me?"

Concentrating on the hunt, I didn't answer her. Up the stairs, around a pillar, towards the edge, and then suddenly over near an archway—the bird dropped her and I aimed. This time Alicia leapt away and I missed. I ran after her. She turned and fired.

Exploding didn't hurt, but it felt weird not to exist on the screen, and—disappointing. Losing even for a second made my excitement sink. So when I came back up on the screen, I was determined. Ruthlessly I chased Alicia down, firing over and over and killing her four more times.

She never hit me again.

By the time the attendant took my helmet off the score was six to one. "That is the most awesome game!" I called to Alicia. Suddenly I noticed a crowd gathered around the pods. Kids were staring at me in a funny way, whispering to each other. Oops—I suddenly remembered that the inter-pod communications link broadcasted our voices over the speaker system. They'd heard everything I said to Alicia. What exactly *had* I said?

Alicia needed to brace herself on the pod as the attendant removed her equipment. "I hated that. Boy, you're really good." Alicia sounded defeated and disgusted. Her face looked pale white and even sick green around the edges. She reminded me of someone in that instant—and I reminded me of someone else.

◆   ◆   ◆

"Debra and Rolph? I didn't know we were going over to their place," I said to Mom.

"We aren't. Debra's working at the Dancing Camel this afternoon and she wanted us to go over there to pick up your present."

"Is it okay if Alicia comes?"

"Oh sure, Alicia can come. Just let your mother know where you're going," Mom told Alicia. Then she turned back to me. "But Beauty can't."

"Aw, I've left her for almost the whole day. Can't she just sit in the car?"

"No. What if we want to have a coke at the restaurant?"

"Can't Beauty come in? Guide dogs are allowed in restaurants, aren't they?"

"Yes. But Beauty's not a guide dog yet."

"Sorry Beauty." I shut her in her crate with Igor and some milk bones.

We picked Dad up from the store, and since he had to make a phone call before leaving we ended up at the Dancing Camel around six o'clock. The restaurant appeared pretty much deserted except for an older couple sipping drinks at the bar and a hockey team seated around their trophy at a table.

"SURPRISE!" Rolph, Debra and Scott stood up front at a microphone. Alicia and Mom and Dad ran up to join them and everyone sang Happy Birthday, even the hockey team. A TV screen mounted near the corner of the ceiling showed some kids blowing out birthday cake candles with the words to Happy Birthday appearing beneath them.

The Dancing Camel is a karaoke bar?" I asked Debra when they'd finished.

"Only some nights, and on every other Saturday evening for teens."

"Which you are now," Rolph chimed in.

"This is great. I *am* suprised."

"It's also Wings night tonight," Debra announced proudly, holding up her hand to a large poster on the wall. A cartoon camel with huge wings emerging from its hump strutted proudly across a cartoon desert.

"You drew that! It's great," Alicia commented. To me she whispered under her breath. "We wanted to invite more people, but they asked me and I didn't know anyone else you liked."

"There isn't anyone. Besides Beauty." I chewed my lip and vowed again to be friendlier.

"It doesn't matter," Alicia said. "This is going to be fun!"

"Just look through the songbook and write down the

title and code along with your name for the ones you want to sing," Debra explained.

"No way. Not me. You'll never catch me up there singing."

"Never mind. Here, open your present, quick while Mom's not looking." Holding out a glossy black makeup bag, Debra eyed Mom as she chatted with the karaoke disc jockey. "Better yet, come with me." Debra grabbed my hand and led me to the ladies room. Inside she pulled a chair in front of the mirror. "Here, look," she handed me the bag again.

Inside was a small bottle of liquid foundation, some blush, a lipstick, eyeshadow, an eyeliner pencil, and more mascara. "Wow, this is the greatest."

"And now I'll show you how to use it all."

"Yess!" I answered.

And away she went. She first dabbed and smoothed the ivory liquid all over my face. Miraculously all my freckles faded into the background.

"Close your eyes," she told me as she rubbed a small brush over the eyeshadow palette. I did and could only imagine how the strange shades of green she'd chosen would look on me. "Try to hold still now." Debra stretched my eyelids, one by one, and I felt her draw a line across them. "Here, you can put your own mascara on."

I looked wonderful already. Sophisticated, and with eyes that actually showed for a change. I opened my mouth as I brushed on the mascara.

It took another few minutes for Debra to complete the masterpiece with blush and lipstick. When I walked back out into the dining room, Mom gasped. Scott whistled low under his breath.

I took that as a good sign.

"She looks much too old," Mom complained to Debra.

"She's thirteen, and besides, this is a special occasion."

Mom wanted to say something else, I knew, but Dad smiled at her and in that moment the DJ called out a song and their names. "And now Sarah and Ray Kerr will sing that old Sonny and Cher number, 'I got you, Babe.'"

Up they went. It was a duet. Dad had to sing alone, and then Mom, and then they sang together.

> *They say we're young, we don't have a lot*
> *But at least I'm sure of all the things we've got.*
> *Babe. I got you Babe.*

Mostly they sounded off-key and I wanted to hide for them. But they laughed all the way through the song. "Boy I wish I had their guts," I told Alicia.

Alicia giggled.

Rolph went up to sing "I Can't Help Falling." Not only did he sing well, but he did a great Elvis impression too, curling his lip, swivelling his hips and even wiping a napkin across the back of his neck and tossing it to Debra.

Rolph took the microphone from the stand, strutted over to where Debra sat and knelt down in front of her, grabbing her hand as he sang the chorus. I remembered how he had blown her up at the Virtual Reality game, and instead of hating him for it now, I felt embarrassed. It was only a game, wasn't it? I looked at Alicia and promised myself I would make it up to her.

Scott belted out a hard rock number and even Alicia did a good job on a Madonna song.

They all looked like they were having such fun, I secretly wished I'd put my name down for something.

By the time we ate the birthday cake it was nine o'clock

and the restaurant was starting to get crowded. "We better be going soon," Mom said.

"Elizabeth Kerr for 'It's My Party,'" the DJ called out.

"He didn't call Elizabeth Kerr, did he?" I asked, startled. "I never put down any songs on the sheet."

Alicia grinned at me. "We put your name in while you were getting your makeover in the washroom."

"Go on! Be a good sport!" Scott nudged me.

What choice did I have? I ran up and took the microphone the DJ handed me. There was a screen at my feet and the words appeared highlighted in red just when I was supposed to sing them. I looked around at all the faces in the room and missed the first few bars. Then I cleared my throat and took a deep breath and sang. With the background music and the microphone in my hand, I suddenly felt that I didn't sound all that bad. I started to sway and do movements to the music too.

"All right Elizabeth!" I heard Scott call out.

Was this really me? I caught sight of myself in a side mirror. Amazing—it was as though someone had finally moved me ahead from pause-frame childhood. Taller, older, and maybe confident even, it sure didn't look like me. I felt powerful.

The song ended and I stepped down from the small stage. I looked at Scott and Alicia, Mom and Dad and Debra and Rolph. I felt a rush of love and happiness. *This is a really weird year*, I thought and then looked in the mirror again—the new me. I decided to become that new person.

Chapter 23

It was the first warm day of May and we were eating barbecued hamburgers at the picnic table outside—a happy easy meal—so why did Mom seem so down? "You know, I was thinking," Mom said.

"I hate when you do that," Dad interrupted, but he smiled. Putting all the fixings on his burger, Dad didn't notice the expression on Mom's face.

"No, you'll like this," Mom continued. "Since Debra's started living with Rolph, there haven't been nearly as many arguments at the table."

"I miss that," Dad said.

Mom made a face at him. "Sure you do. Anyway, I don't think we always have to share only good news at supper. Maybe that puts too much pressure on us. We should just talk about anything. When we're all together for a meal, it's the perfect time to share everything, bad news included."

I heard something in the tone of Mom's voice, something that made my heart pound a little harder.

"Just when I have some good news for a change," Dad said. He still wasn't noticing.

"You can share it with us, by all means."

"Regal Trust called me this afternoon."

"You're kidding, Dad."

"No. They want me to come back to work as part of the Disaster Recovery team. They're about to implement the project."

"What about your job at Futures?" I asked.

"And your computer-buying seminars?" Mom added. "You love teaching."

"I'm just going back as a consultant on this project . . . at least for now."

"You think they'll want you back permanently?" Mom asked.

"Yes, I do."

"Well, that's wonderful." Mom didn't sound sure though.

"It's nice to be wanted." Dad blinked hard and fast twice. It was the twitch, back again after all these months.

I wondered about that twitch and Mom's strangeness while I arranged the pickle slices on my second hamburger. Then I pushed it out of my mind as I took a bite. "I've got good news too."

"Could you wait until your mouth is empty to tell us please?"

I nodded.

"This is extraordinary. As soon as I give up on an idea, it begins to work." Mom shook her head. "What's your good news?"

"I got an A on my Pillow Pet in Family Studies."

"Elizabeth! You've improved in sewing then," Dad commented.

"Actually Jessica helped me a lot." It had been Alicia's suggestion and I'd gone along with it. Something about sewing eyes and tusks on a pillow made it hard not to become friends.

"Which reminds me," Mom interrupted. "She called earlier. Wants you to call her back. Something about a sleepover."

"Oh good, it's on then!" Talking about guys and trying on makeup didn't seem so stupid any more, now that I was more experienced. "Did Alicia call too?" I asked.

"No but Scott did. He said he'd call back. From now on I'm going to let the answering machine pick up. Every phone call is for you and I'm sick of being your secretary."

"Scott called?" I repeated. I knew there was something on his mind, something he felt guilty about. We were supposed to do things together Friday nights, but more and more often now Scott ended up going out with his friends instead. I could feel myself tensing up. What would it be this time—Monster Trucks again? Beauty nudged me under the table. "Sit down girl. Be careful. You don't want to bump your head on the seat."

"Really, I'm glad you've made so many friends in the last while." The edge was back in Mom's voice. "Because I need to tell you something that you won't think is such good news."

Beauty nuzzled at my knee. I put my hamburger down and patted her head.

"Canine Vision called. They want us to bring Beauty back at the end of the week."

"So soon?" Dad commented. "I thought we'd have her at least a few months more."

Mom shook her head and threw up her hands. Her eyes were shiny with tears she was holding back.

"It's . . . ." Okay was what I wanted to say, but suddenly there was a rock in my throat. I closed my eyes and swallowed down the rock. "Mom?"

"Yes Elizabeth."

"I need to go with her this time. Can I stay home from school that day?"

"Certainly."

After supper I called Scott back.

His voice sounded edgy. "Hi, how's it going, Elizabeth?"

I took a deep breath. "What were you calling about, Scott? Are we still on for Friday?"

"Hey, nothing like that." He sighed a big heavy sigh. I could tell it was much worse.

"Elizabeth, I just wanted to tell you. The grad dance is only for grade eights."

"Mmm," I answered.

"You don't mind, do you? I mean next year we'll be going to different schools." *We should start seeing other people anyway,* that was what he really wanted to say.

Scott would dance with all the girls. He'd clown around. Everyone would love him.

"Are you okay?"

"I'm fine."

"Elizabeth, don't be like this."

"Look, it isn't about your grad dance. Beauty's going back Friday."

"Oh." He sighed. "Aw Elizabeth," he whispered.

It was really hard then because he was quiet and I knew he was feeling badly for me. I swallowed hard. "Scott, there's only a couple of days . . ."

"I have an idea. Why don't I get everyone together at the park, Thursday after supper. That way they can say goodbye to Beauty."

"That's a good idea. And I'll stop in at the Bonds' house tomorrow so Marnie can see Beauty one last time too."

I wanted to hold the sun up in the sky that night and to hold it down the next morning, to slow down the seconds that flashed by, to hold on to Beauty forever. But I couldn't.

Beauty loved visiting Marnie the next day. Even though Beauty was so much bigger now, she loped around with Marnie as if she were the same puppy who fell in the fish tank back in September. It made me smile to think about that now.

"Can I give Beauty a toffee?" Marnie asked as we were heading out the door. The candy lay unwrapped in her hand and she was already bent over ready to release it to Beauty.

"No Marnie. Beauty's going to be a special dog. She's not allowed people food."

Marnie stared at me and then straightened. Finally she seemed to understand. "Here, you have it then." She placed the sticky toffee in my hand. "Goodbye Beauty."

On Thursday Beauty seemed to sense my mood and even she walked heavy-pawed and slow towards the park. From a distance I saw Scott hanging from the monkey bars, and stopped to watch him while he still couldn't see me.

He was grinning upside down at Vicky, who was sitting on a rung lower, laughing back at him. He held out his hand to her as if to encourage her to try a similar stunt. Finally he sat up and helped her hitch her legs on a bar. She seemed hesitant to drop her body. "Don't worry, I'll hold you!" I heard his words tossed on the wind as he climbed down. Finally, Vicky hung upside down, Scott's arms around her waist.

I touched the locket around my neck. "You win, Scott," I said softly. I would always have a part of him in my heart anyway, even if it was only the close-up of his nose and eyes in the locket. I stayed back for an extra moment. When Alicia, Todd, Jessica, and Lydia joined Scott, I finally walked over.

Alicia and Todd weren't officially going out yet. They just looked at each other a lot and laughed really hard at everything. "Can I throw Beauty's stick for her?" Alicia asked at the same time as Todd. They both reached for the stick, touching each other's hands for the longest time as they decided who would throw first. A few months ago that might have made me uncomfortable, but now I felt happy for Alicia. She was at the beginning of something instead of at the end like Scott and me.

Lydia and Jessica each threw the stick for Beauty. And Scott and Vicky. Each time Beauty returned it with a huge happy doggie grin, even for Vicky.

"Beauty loves doing stuff for people," Scott offered, trying to make me feel better.

So did Scott, I realized. Making the guys let me play Rollerblade hockey, cheering me up when I was down, and not breaking up with me when I was already losing Beauty.

"Yeah I guess." He was trying to make me feel better but it wasn't working.

We all just hung around awhile then, sitting on the grass and talking, patting Beauty and watching the sun set.

"How long before she gets her new owner?" Scott asked.

"Probably about six months. First they train her, and then they pair her with a blind person and they train together."

"Maybe once Beauty has her new owner you can visit her," Alicia said.

"People come from all over to get guide dogs. Beauty could be going to Alberta for all we know. Besides, visiting would be hard for me."

"Would you do it again?" Vicky asked. "I mean, raise a foster puppy?"

"I don't think I can."

"Elizabeth, it'll be okay, you'll see," Scott said when

Beauty and I got up to leave.

I looked straight into Scott's soft brown eyes and tried to smile. "Maybe after a while."

It was a late night but I set my alarm early so that Beauty and I would have extra time together. After everyone else was asleep I snuck Beauty up to my bed, wrapped my arms around her and shut my eyes. Thump, thump, thump, thump, the rhythm of her heartbeat soothed me to sleep.

Next morning, the alarm and Beauty's tongue seemed to go off at the same time. "Okay girl, okay. I'm getting up." I dressed quickly and we headed downstairs together.

Dad was already sitting at the table peeling a banana as I fed Beauty. He was wearing his Disaster Recovery shirt.

"Back to Regal Trust today, eh Dad?" I said finally. I grabbed a banana from the fruit bowl and peeled it too. We both stuffed the fruit in our mouths at the same time and chewed silently.

"Yeah. Today's a tough day for you too, eh princess?" Beauty walked over to Dad and he stroked her gently.

I couldn't answer.

"Do me a favour. You're heading outside, aren't you?"

I nodded.

"Take that container of kitchen scraps and our banana peels and dump it in the compost."

"Sure Dad. Outside, girl." Beauty followed me to the back corner of the yard. I lifted the lid and the bugs scuttled away as I dumped the container.

Beauty nosed wildly around at the side of the compost.

"What is it, girl?"

She lifted her head and I saw a long fat earthworm slither from the bottom of the compost bin. I slid the side panel near it upwards to open the bin. Black, black earth tumbled out.

"Topsoil," I told Beauty. "One of Mom's family projects finally worked." I slid the panel closed.

We ran around the yard till we were both panting. Then Beauty and I sprawled in front of the TV and watched three Sesame Street reruns back to back. It made me feel as though I was five years old again, which was what I needed. We were watching Mr. Dressup when Mom called for us.

"Time to go, Elizabeth."

I grabbed some dog treats from the cupboard in case I needed to bribe Beauty to leave with the trainer.

It was a half-hour drive and the happiest passenger in the van was Beauty, looking out the window, wagging her tail in my face.

"It's going to be all right Beauty. You'll see." Beauty didn't listen, but I needed to tell her. We rolled into the parking lot and I saw a woman walking in the back with a golden retriever.

Beauty's ears perked up.

"You're going into training just like that dog. You'll like that won't you, girl?" Beauty lathered my face, and then we walked into the building.

A couple of black Labs passed us with their trainers. Just like Beauty, they were eager and happy. Maybe this wouldn't be so bad. If Beauty could deal with it, I could force myself to deal with it too.

"Down the hall here is the puppy coordinator's office," Mom motioned. She knocked and a woman opened the door.

"Come in, Mrs. Kerr. Elizabeth? Hello, I'm Dawn Ferris." She shook my clammy hand. "There isn't much left for you to do. I have a few forms."

"Can I say goodbye to her?" I asked Mom.

"We can take a walk, Mrs. Kerr, so Elizabeth has a few moments."

Mom nodded and they left.

Beauty looked puzzled at the door after it closed.

"Beauty, I'm going to miss you so much. You're a good, good dog. And . . . I love you." I wasn't going to cry, not as long as Beauty stayed this happy, grinning and wagging her tail. I stopped patting her and wiped under my eyes. That's when she nudged me with her head and placed her paw on my arm. The weight was comforting. I took her paw and shook it. "Friends forever, Beauty. Just remember that wherever you are." I got down on my knees and hugged her. She washed my face with her flapjack tongue.

The door opened again. "Ready to go, Beauty?" I released her and Dawn snapped a lead on Beauty's collar. "Come Beauty."

Beauty never looked back. I watched her wagging tail disappear out the door and I tried to smile.

"I'm almost finished filling out this form," Mom said.

I looked around at the pictures on the wall of the office. All the teams of dogs and owners who had graduated from the centre hung there. This was going to be all right, I told myself. This was going to be all right.

And that's when I heard her. It started as a whining with a few yips and yaps in it. Then it grew into a whimpering that turned into full-blown howling, sort of a cross between a baby and a very sad wolf. I covered my ears and tried to ignore it. One long howl, now, penetrated into my bones, and then another. Just like that first time when I was in the tub. Only this time I couldn't go and get her from the crate. Mom and I just walked away.

Chapter 24

"If you don't start eating soon, you won't be able to see Debra and Rolph off at the airport."

It had been three days since we'd left Beauty crying and howling. My stomach had turned from an aching solid to a churning mass that wouldn't accept food.

"She didn't understand, Mom. She thought I'd just abandoned her."

"Oh no, I'm sure that's not true."

"I can't forget her crying. I keep hearing it."

"Elizabeth, do you remember when you first started babysitting Marnie?"

"Sure, it was awful."

"Yes. Each time her parents left Marnie would cry, first for hours, then for half an hour, and then for less, and now what does she do?"

"She just grabs for my babysitting kit."

"Exactly. She didn't understand about her parents leaving in the beginning but then she came to understand."

"But Mom, I'm never going back for Beauty, ever."

"That's true. But you know how she loves people. When Beauty gets paired with her new owner, I think she'll come to understand."

"If only I could know that."

"Maybe this will help. Dawn called, you remember she's the puppy coordinator?"

"Uh huh."

"Well, she told me how well Beauty performed on her latest assessment."

"Did she say whether Beauty had stopped howling?"

"Of course she's stopped. Dawn told me that Beauty would always remember her first owner, though. Always, Elizabeth."

"Uh huh."

"She also asked me if we would raise another puppy for them." Mom searched my face for a moment.

"I can't. Not yet, anyway."

Mom nodded. "Do you think you could hold down some dry toast?"

"Could I have some Chocotella on it?"

"Mmm. Perhaps just a dab."

"When is Debra's flight?"

"Tomorrow at three o'clock in the afternoon."

"Mom?"

"Yes Elizabeth."

"I can eat in the kitchen."

"Good. Let me help you out of bed."

While I was sipping at some flat ginger ale, Dad walked in. Still wearing his Disaster Recovery shirt, he now sported a half an inch worth of stubble and his eyes looked red and bleary.

"Dad, is this the first time you've been home since Beauty left?"

"Yes. But I did catch a few hours of shut-eye in between system crashes."

"How did it go, Ray?"

"Terrible. I told them it wouldn't work and it didn't. They want me back. Can I have some of whatever Elizabeth's eating?"

Mom squinted at Dad. "Chocotella sandwich. You must be starving."

"And tired. I'm never getting up again."

"Better hurry to bed then. Tomorrow Debra and Rolph are leaving."

Dad hit his hand against his forehead. "I've lost all track of time."

The toast stayed down and Dad got some rest. But the next day neither of us felt a hundred percent as we headed into the waiting room of the airport. Debra and Rolph carried only a couple of bags each and Debra seemed so excited to be flying away to a new life that she reminded me of Beauty when we drove her back to the Centre. Would she cry later too? I felt like howling myself. Inside everything was heavy, heavy and my eyes, throat and head ached dully.

"Flight 404 to Los Angeles now boarding at Gate 6. Flight 404."

"That's us," Debra spoke out gaily.

Mom hugged her tightly. "Please look into that school. If only to humour me."

"Mom!"

Mom's face started to crack and I could see her mouth quiver.

"I promise, Mom. I promise."

"I can't help thinking that if I hadn't put your laundry away that day, you'd still be our little girl living at home." Dad folded his arms around Debra.

"Dad. That's not true."

"Do great things, Debra," he told her softly and then

~ 191 ~

hugged her tightly. When he turned away, he sniffled. "Do you have a Kleenex, Sarah? I think I'm coming down with something."

"No, I use a cloth handkerchief now." She passed him what looked like a large white surrender flag and Dad blew into it noisily.

It was my turn. "Debra, there's something I have to tell you."

"Last call for Flight 404, now boarding at gate 6. Flight 404."

"What is it, Liz? Hurry, there's no time."

"It's about your art project. Beauty and I dropped mascara on it and I painted over it but it smudged and well, it was really great and you should have gotten A+ or S+, whatever the top mark is. It was all our fault that you didn't. I think you're a fantastic artist."

"I love you too, Liz. I didn't like the teacher and he didn't like me. It had nothing to do with your smudge. But thank you. I'm not quitting art. I just quit school." Looking over to Mom she added, "For a while."

We walked them over to their gate and watched as their bags cleared through the metal detector. Debra grabbed her bag and then turned to us one last time, her eyes shining. She raised her hand and formed a V with her fingers.

Mom waved back frantically and then put her hand to her mouth when Rolph and Debra disappeared down a long passageway.

We returned to our parking level where we could hear the thunder of planes taking off and landing. "Just a minute," I told Mom. "I want to see if I can find Debra's plane." I ran to the railing and peered over. There were about a million red tractor trucks dragging wagons of luggage around the tarmac. I saw a small airplane being towed from its parking spot by a white truck. "Is that it?" I asked Mom. She ran over with Dad, who still dabbed at his nose with Mom's handkerchief.

"Yes, at least that's the airline." Mom bundled her sweater tightly around herself and shivered. The wind blew in cold at us from all the open sides of the parking level. "Can we go now?"

"I can't believe she's really leaving." Dad stared out at the plane as it began its slow crawl towards the runway.

"Let's stay," I begged Mom.

We stood there, glumly watching as the plane crawled away from the tow truck. The engine whined and lights flashed on its wings as the plane taxied out to the runway. Slowly first, then picking up speed and then . . . the plane suddenly broke away from the ground, rising higher and higher.

"Live long and prosper," I whispered softly.

Dad continued to battle his case of the sniffles as we headed for the van. When he blew his nose a second time, Mom and I looked at each other. "You better let me drive, Ray. Till you've had more sleep."

We piled in and a heavy silence settled over the van. Instinctively, I reached to pat at the empty space at my side and a wave of loneliness swept over me.

Dad went to bed when we got home and Mom made us a pot of tea. We sat at the kitchen table, Mom staring straight ahead, stirring her cup, clinkety-clink, clinkety-clink, not saying anything.

"Did you know the compost pile made some soil?"

"Hmm? What's that?"

"Your compost project," I repeated. "It's working. There's all black soil and worms at the bottom."

Mom smiled. "Just when I give up, things start to work. I told you so."

"Mom."

"Yes Elizabeth," she answered tonelessly.

"I didn't like Rolph at first and I'm still not sure he's my favourite person in the world. But he loves Debra."

Mom's lower lips pursed. "You're probably right."

"It's hard isn't it?" I asked her.

"What's that?"

"It's just like Beauty. I knew she would grow up and I'd have to give her away. Debra and you, it's like that, isn't it?"

"Yes, I suppose it is." Mom scraped back her chair and trudged over to her bulletin board. She looked at her list of things to do and sighed. With the pen on the string she scrawled something across it. Her shoulders slumped forward. "I think I need to lie down, Elizabeth. Maybe we'll order out later."

"Sure Mom." She looked so sad and defeated as she headed up the stairs that I wanted to do something for her. But what? I glanced around the kitchen and saw an empty Chocotella jar still gooey with its remains.

Well, I can at least clean that out, I thought and filled the sink with soapy water, soaking the jar along with our tea cups and other assorted dishes lying around. What else? I could make supper. I opened the fridge and took out a couple of cucumbers and tomatoes. A steak lay in the meat compartment, and I pulled that out too. Baked potatoes with that, maybe, and I reached again into the vegetable bin. Once I'd peeled the cucumbers, I stuck the cool strips of the skin across my forehead, nose, and chin. It felt good, even though the strips began falling off almost instantly. After soaking awhile, the Chocotella jar just needed a couple of swishes with the washcloth and it was ready for the Blue Box. The potato and cucumber skins I dumped into the compost bin. The microwave hummed, the steak sizzled under the grill, the salad sat ready on the table. Anything else, I wondered and headed for the bulletin board to check. *Unsatisfactory!* the large loopy letters scribbled across the list read. 10/30!

Quickly I ticked all the supper items off the list—they were all done. Load the laundry, I'd do that now. Vacuum living room, wash floor, clean bathroom. I couldn't do all of it before supper or even today. Instead I just initialled the jobs. Poor Mom, if I couldn't finish the twenty jobs left on the list, how had she ever planned on getting all thirty done?

I carefully wiped off Mom's "Unsatisfactory" and her score. Then I wrote:

> *10/10 Excellent! You don't have to do it all by yourself any more.*
>
> *Love Elizabeth*

Chapter 25

They say that with time you get over losing someone. I found it wasn't true. In the months that followed, Beauty became like a missing part of my body. I pined for her. Maybe if she'd died, it would have been easier. But she hadn't. And in my mind, over and over, I heard her howling from a cage. I'd told her goodbye, but Beauty had never understood well enough to say goodbye to me. Like a dangling telephone receiver, I felt I needed to be hung up somehow.

I thought about her less as the months went by, but only because I had lots of other things to think about.

Scott and I remained friends even when he started high school. We had stopped kissing and holding hands pretty much the night of Beauty's goodbye party in the park. Scott told me about his new girlfriend as we played Rollerblade hockey one Saturday, the first time in about six months. I ignored the tightening in my throat. I didn't want him as that kind of boyfriend any more, he was too familiar, too much like a cousin or brother, and I knew his faults too well. Still, it hurt. I never wanted to lose someone again so I skated out of goals, body-checked him and nabbed the puck. "Concentrate on the game, Scott," I told him. "You're losing."

Dad never returned to Regal Trust and worked strictly as a consultant on certain projects. He didn't ever want to give over his entire life to them again.

Mom became a full-time English instructor for day classes, which meant she got to teach Creative Writing and a short story workshop as well as remedial and introductory college English. Dad and I both took on a share of the chores on Mom's bulletin board list.

Every day Mom and I rushed to check the mail for letters from Debra. She asked me to mail her the Dancing Camel posters and menus I'd inherited from her apartment. She didn't explain why, and I hated parting with them, but I figured I owed it to Debra after ruining her first design project.

At Christmas we flew to Los Angeles, but not for the wedding. Debra and Rolph were postponing that until the spring when they could have it outdoors back here, where most of their friends and family lived.

The trip was the family Christmas present that Dad decided Mom and I needed. He was right. First time on a plane, first time seeing a real live palm tree, first time in Hollywood—every minute was exciting. Disneyland was almost better than snow. Rolph took us on a special tour of the place where he worked and got us passes to some attractions.

The most exciting moment had to be when we unwrapped our Christmas presents from Debra and Rolph. We all received the same package. Flat and wide, I instantly recognized it to be a book. A book? What kind of book would she possibly think we would all like?

I opened mine up. The first thing I noticed was the cover picture, a camel smiling as it stood on a skateboard.

"Illustrations by Debra Kerr," was the second thing I

noticed. It was a children's picture book. I pored through it, studying all of Debra's camels. "I love it, I love it, I love it," I told her.

"This is extraordinary," Mom gasped. "How did it all come about?"

"Rolph heard from a friend that the original illustrator couldn't meet his deadline. The editor was frantic." Debra tossed off the words casually as though they meant nothing to her, but her face glowed Debra-style. We all needed sunglasses.

"That's why you needed your menus back," I said.

"We're so proud of you." Dad turned the pages of his copy slowly, running his fingers over the pictures.

"The book doesn't do justice to the paintings. Come see them hanging on Debra's studio wall." Rolph beamed as he showed us.

"I had to work so quickly, I didn't have time for anything else. I still haven't looked into taking courses. But I will, Mom. There's so much more I want to learn about art."

Eyes shining, Mom held the book closely to her heart. Her receiver had been hung up at that moment.

Even though the trip was supposed to be our only Christmas present, Dad also gave me his Disaster Recovery sweatshirt.

"Thanks Dad. I've always loved this shirt."

"Maybe it will bring you good luck."

I shrugged my shoulders. Nothing would bring Beauty back, but maybe it would bring me courage.

Mr. Swanson had collected the mail for us every day while we were away. When we arrived home, among the assortment of bills and Christmas cards was an envelope from Canine Vision Canada.

"That came the very first day you were gone," Mr. Swanson told us.

It was an invitation. Beauty was graduating and we were invited to the ceremony.

"The date is tomorrow—I'd better call right away. How about it, Elizabeth?" Mom asked. "Do you think you can handle it?"

"No. But I have to go anyway, Mom."

I dressed the next morning in all my special favourite clothes. I wore the black leather pants and silk shirt I'd inherited from Debra topped with Dad's Disaster Recovery sweatshirt. While searching under the bed for my purple desert boots, I came across Igor. It wasn't the same monster Beauty had first snatched from Debra's room. You could see where she had sewn the legs and arms back and the polyester fur was worn off in a few places. Still, after brushing off the dust bunnies, I hugged Igor to me.

It was a different kind of trip for me. I noticed things with a slow clearness this time: the German shepherd mat at the door with the Canine Vision slogan, "They'll never walk alone," the rug hooking of a yellow Lab dog hanging on the wall, thank you letters from school children who'd been on a visit, framed photographs of graduating guide dog and human classes. They all reminded me of when Mom had first told us about the project. How noble and worthwhile we'd thought it was.

Then a puppy and her trainer passed us in the hall. The dog bounded happily ahead, her tongue hanging out, her tail wagging. Innocent and trusting, the dog was the noble one, I thought. It was her sacrifice and she'd never had a chance to choose.

Dawn greeted us and brought us to the lounge.

"Is Beauty in here?" I asked.

"She should be. Sue Williams is her new owner. She's a middle-aged woman about my height, black hair, dark eyes. You go ahead and introduce yourself, I have to see about the others."

There were two tables set up with refreshments, a coffee machine, some pop cans, a few plates of sandwiches and doughnuts. A woman helped herself to coffee and at her feet was a black Labrador. I held my breath.

When they both faced me, I realized it wasn't Beauty.

Seated around four other tables were all kinds of people but I didn't pay any attention to them. I was too busy scanning the dogs at their feet. Three more black Labradors, none of which were Beauty, and two golden retrievers.

My heart pounded hard against my chest. Where was she? I spotted some more dogs sprawled on the floor near the couches. Wrong colour—they were yellow Labs.

"Don't worry," Mom told me. "She's here somewhere. Go get yourself a doughnut."

With Igor tucked under my arm, it was awkward but I picked out a chocolate dip doughnut and an orange pop. That's when she walked in.

I didn't notice right away, but when I did I couldn't believe how much she'd changed. Tall, slim and yes, beautiful, Beauty turned towards me. Her caramel eyes looked straight into mine and her tail wagged. As she walked closer, I didn't know what to do. I wanted to call out, but wasn't sure if that would be disturbing her in her new job.

Finally I walked over to meet Beauty and her new owner.

"Ms. Williams, hi I'm Elizabeth." I reached out my hand and in that moment forgot about Igor. As he dropped, I grabbed to catch him but lost my chocolate dip. It fell to the floor and rolled over directly beneath Beauty's nose.

"No Beauty," I said softly. But I didn't have to. She looked down at it and then looked back at me.

"Good girl," I told her. "I'm sorry Ms. Williams, I just dropped my doughnut."

"And Beauty resisted. What a good dog."

I picked up the chocolate dip and watched as Ms. Williams smiled and patted Beauty. Then she reached into her purse and handed Beauty a milk bone. It was something I might have done, and it felt strange to have someone else reward my dog. But of course she wasn't my dog any more. It also felt good to know Ms. Williams treated Beauty the same way I did. "Let's grab a chair and get acquainted, shall we?" Ms. Williams suggested.

"Uh, my mother's over there on the couch." Without thinking I pointed, and then quickly dropped my hand when I remembered she couldn't see. "That's straight ahead, Ms. Williams."

"Call me Sue, please," she told me. "Maybe I'll just get a coffee over here first then. Left Beauty, forward."

I walked beside her and almost stopped when I noticed a heating vent on the floor.

Beauty didn't though—she moved straight across it. I felt so proud of her.

When Sue and I finally sat down beside Mom on the couch, I realized I still had Igor tucked under my armpit. The monster seemed so worn out and ugly, I almost felt embarrassed to give it to Sue now.

"I brought Beauty's favourite stuffed animal. It's pretty wrecked, but, maybe she'd like it as a souvenir?" I held it out to Sue.

"Thank you. I'm glad to hear she likes stuffed animals. My children have a ton."

"Children?" I asked. I guess I'd never thought about blind people having children.

"Yes, I have Julie who's about your age and Jeff, he's ten and Kelly who's five."

"Beauty loves kids," I said. "I took her babysitting all the time. She went out on Halloween with me and she loves playing in the park."

"Dawn told me all about you. What a wonderful job you'd done with Beauty. I can't tell you how much it means to me." Sue's soft brown eyes didn't focus on me, or anything for that matter, but still they seemed to smile, friendly and warm at the whole world. Her hair was the same colour as Beauty's fur and she was tall and slim also. In a bizarre way they looked alike, as though they belonged together.

"Did Dawn tell me you were a programmer?" Mom asked Sue.

"Yes, Beauty will take me to work every day at the Royal Bank."

She's a programmer, like Dad. A regular person, a mom and a worker, I couldn't believe I'd never thought about things like that before. "Can I pat Beauty?" I asked hesitantly.

"Oh sure, I'm sorry. Let me take off Beauty's harness. Just a second, there, now she can play."

Beauty shook her body along with her tail. When I dropped down to my knees on the floor, she threw herself at me. I hugged her and she licked my face over and over.

I stayed on the floor the rest of our visit. Dawn presented us with a graduation certificate that had a picture of Sue and Beauty on it. I read the words underneath the picture:

Canine Vision Canada
hereby expresses its gratitude
to the Kerr Family
for a meaningful contribution
ensuring that
"They'll Never Walk Alone."

"I'm going to hang this on your Dog of Fame wall," I told Beauty. "You understand now, don't you girl?" I hugged her tightly. "You were my best friend when I needed you most. Now someone else needs you more." Pulling away from Beauty, I felt her furry leg brush against my face. I held out my hand and shook her paw for the last time. Then I stood up as Sue hitched the harness back on her.

Beauty wanted to walk away with me when Mom and I started for the door. "No Beauty. Stay!" Her tail waved once and then it hung back down. Mom and I headed quickly for the exit. I couldn't resist turning around and looking at Beauty one last time.

She was still standing there staring at me with her tail hanging down. "Goodbye, Beauty."

Beauty lifted her ears slightly and waved her tail. This time I felt sure she knew she was waving goodbye.

This time she understood. Click.

♦   ♦   ♦

"Mom, I'd like to do it again."

"Elizabeth, really? You became so attached to Beauty, it made you sick to give her up."

"It isn't easy. But it's . . ." I stopped and searched for the right word in my head. "Meaningful" was what I settled on, Debra's word, the word on the certificate.

"All right, Elizabeth."

Dawn was delighted. "I have the perfect puppy for you. She's available right now."

I waited in her office for Beauty II.

"She's a little younger and she's a chocolate Lab."

I didn't listen any more. A wobbly dark brown puppy with a pink nose waddled over to me. I cuddled her and she nipped at my hand with needle-sharp teeth.

"Don't," I complained. "That hurts."

"RAWF," she answered, leaping up and washing my face with her flapjack tongue. I accepted her apology, scratching behind her ears. Suddenly she placed her paw on my arm and it felt so much like Beauty that tears came to my eyes.

"Friends," I said softly, taking the furry size thirteen paw into my hand and shaking it. "We can be friends," I explained, knowing Beauty II wouldn't understand. "But I'm not going to love you." Even as she licked the tears from my cheeks I knew it was a promise I could never keep.

Presents

Great Inspirational Romance at a Great Price!

Heartsong Presents books are inspirational romances in contemporary and historical settings, designed to give you an enjoyable, spirit-lifting reading experience. You can choose wonderfully written titles from some of today's best authors like Andrea Boeshaar, Wanda E. Brunstetter, Yvonne Lehman, Joyce Livingston, and many others.

When ordering quantities less than twelve, above titles are $2.97 each.
Not all titles may be available at time of order.